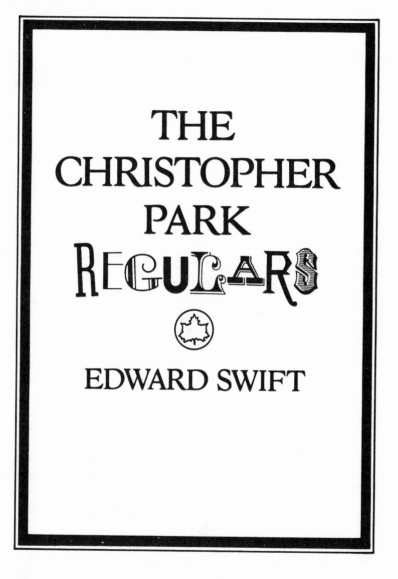

THE
CHRISTOPHER
PARK
REGULARS

EDWARD SWIFT

Also by E. Swift

A Place with Promise
Principia Martindale
Splendora

THE
CHRISTOPHER
PARK
REGULARS

A Novel

**BRITISH
AMERICAN
PUBLISHING**

The characters in this book are ficticious.
Only the park exists.

I would like to express my gratitude to The Helene
Wurlitzer Foundation of New Mexico, the MacDowell
Colony, and the New York Foundation for the Arts.

Published by British American Publishing
3 Cornell Road
Latham, NY 12110
Manufactured in the United States of America

93 92 91 90 89 5 4 3 2 1

Library of Congress Cataloging in Publication Data

Swift, Edward, 1943—
    The Christopher Park regulars.

    I. Title.
PS3569.W483C47 1989   813'.54   88–35264
ISBN 0–945167–16–4

To my cousin
Dana Pullen-Hall

CONTENTS

THE CHRISTOPHER PARK REGULARS

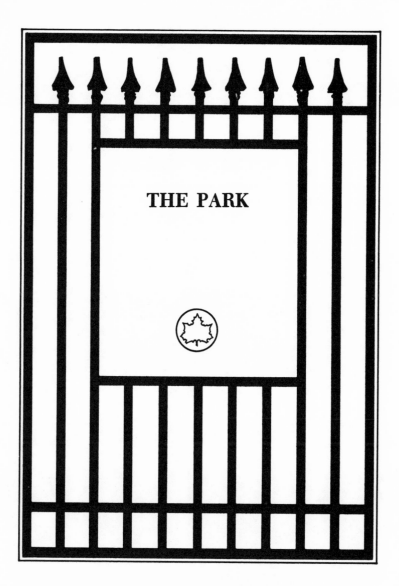

THE PARK

Christopher Park, a small triangle of benches and trees enclosed by an iron fence with three gates, is, oddly enough for Greenwich Village, bordered by four streets: West Fourth, along with a sliver of Seventh Avenue South, Christopher Street, and Grove Street. The gate at the main entrance is graced with a vine-covered arch, but the other two gates are unadorned, and sometimes all three are locked for an entire day. When that happens the police officer in charge of opening the park each morning is met with severe reprimands by a handful of regular benchsitters. These devoted few, the Christopher Park regulars, expect all three gates to be open when they arrive, usually by late morning or early afternoon, and to remain open until midnight. For the most part they reserve their benchsitting to the warm months, but some of them, Andrew T. Andrews for one, and C.C. Wake for another, will often

3

brave the coldest days of winter; Andrew, to work on his epic novel-in-progress; C.C. Wake, to answer the public telephone located near the main entrance.

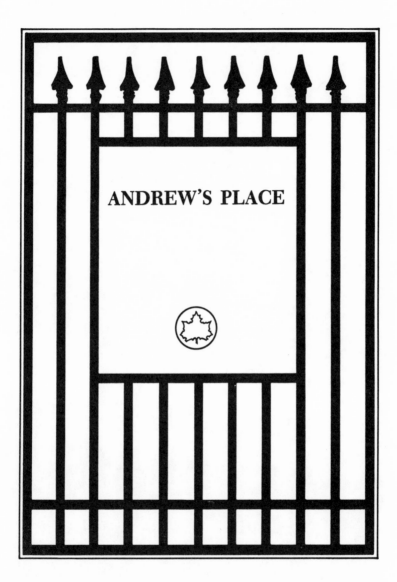

ANDREW'S PLACE

On the first warm day of the year Andrew T. Andrews sharpened his pencils until they were all the same length. Then he capped each one with a new eraser and tested the points against his wrist. They were very sharp, and that made him feel secure. "I am ready to write the truth," he said as he left his Bleecker Street apartment. His pencils were in one hand, his notebook in the other, and a wadded-up dollar bill along with his house keys made his left leg feel heavier than the right one. That bothered him. He felt out of balance, and didn't know what to do about it. "I'll be all right once I sit down," he assured himself. At Christopher Park, not to be confused with the nearby Sheridan Square, Andrew sat on his favorite bench and began scribbling in his spiral notebook. He was relieved to be able to pick up exactly where he left off the day before. Suddenly his world seemed balanced once again.

At the age of forty-eight Andrew had completed

two unpublished novels and was determined to become a famous writer. "With a name like Andrew T. Andrews, how can I fail?" He held tenaciously to this point of view.

His first book was about himself. His second book was about himself, and his work-in-progress pursued the same theme. Yet he insisted that he was not writing a trilogy. "I am displaying the full range of human propensities and probabilities." That's how he sometimes described what he was doing.

Andrew T. Andrews was what some people still called "Old Manhattan." Born on the Upper East Side, he had spent his summers on Long Island and had attended boarding school in Connecticut. At Yale he majored in mathematics. At MIT he received a masters and a Ph.D. in mechanical engineering. Then he married a woman from Boston and returned to New York where he went to work for a prestigious consulting firm in the financial district. His father, a successful surgeon, had urged him to accept the position. Dr. Andrews had also encouraged his only son to move into a townhouse on East Sixty-sixth Street. But what Andrew really wanted to do all along was to live in artistic poverty while writing a great novel, or better still, several of them.

Twenty-four years later, immediately after the death of his father, Andrew left his job, his wife, and his twin daughters, who were graduating from Harvard. He packed one suitcase with three changes of clothes as well as a coffee pot, a cup, a plate, and a frying pan. "This is all I'll ever need," he said when he left East Sixty-sixth Street and moved to the Village. "For the rest of my life I intend to devote every minute of my time to writing."

Three years and two books later he considered himself an undiscovered success. His family considered him a problem. The regulars in Christopher Park tried not to consider him at all.

"I am almost ready for exposure," he assured himself on that first warm day of the year when Christopher Park was suddenly filled with familiar faces, and Andrew, although he rarely spoke to the regulars, was aware of their presence and was hoping they were taking the time to admire his display of artistic discipline. That day he was dressed in a new, carefully chosen outfit, an "Art for Art's Sake" sweatshirt with baggy, white pants from the paint store and tennis shoes worn without socks or laces. His eyes were magnified by hornrimmed glasses; stemless, they were held to the bridge of his nose by shoestrings wrapped around his ears and tied under his chin. His new haircut, short on the sides and long on the top, was designed to elongate his face, and it did.

Andrew lived alone in three rooms on the second floor of a tenement on Bleecker Street. His windows were covered with sheets, and a bare mattress was on the floor. He hardly ever swept, cooked, or washed his clothes. Sometimes he even forced himself to starve.

"On Bleecker Street I have learned to recognize my true voice as it appears on the printed, that is to say, the handwritten as well as the type-written, page." He wrote this in the margin of his spiral notebook. He had no idea how he would use the sentence in his novel, but something told him that he would eventually find a place for it.

From the beginning of his writing career Andrew had enjoyed working in public, and that day was no exception. It pleased him to know that someone might be watching, that someone might be trying to guess his subject matter. But it displeased him to be interrupted, so he always isolated himself from everyone else by sitting on a bench that the Parks Department never bothered to clean. Pigeons roosted in a plane tree that shaded the bench, and their droppings dirtied all but a small space at one end. That's where Andrew usually sat. He could be alone there. The pigeon droppings put distance between him and the next person.

The next person was Cherokee Rose. She was eighty-nine years old and had published one novel, entitled *Neither Here Nor There*. The book was

1,915 pages and no longer available, even at the Strand.

That afternoon Cherokee was wearing what she called her Cherry Orchard skirt. It came from the Circle Rep, was ankle length and dark blue. Her Ukrainian blouse had lots of yellow on it, and her Chinese slippers were black and gold with green dragons. Her long, red hair had just been shampooed and was dripping wet. While it dried in the sun, she smoked filterless cigarettes and read the *National Enquirer.* "This is the only newspaper in America that's brave enough to print the truth," she told Andrew.

To him she was just a familiar face and not a name. He had never heard of her book, which took forty-five years to complete, and, although he was vaguely aware of being addressed, he did not acknowledge her presence. He was too busy writing about his life in the crib. His last five pages were filled with mathematical formulas expressed in baby talk and nursery rhymes. "I'm trying to create a new language," he kept telling himself.

The High Fiber Man, the thirty-four-year-old heir to a breakfast cereal fortune, was sitting on a row of benches lining the other side of the park. Presently he got up and approached Cherokee, who was staring into space.

"Can I have a light?" he asked.

"No! Because you interrupted me while I was thinking." Cherokee slid a book of matches under her voluminous skirt.

"Shhh," said Andrew, without making eye contact.

The High Fiber Man was dressed in a dusty tuxedo and Red Ball tennis shoes, his daily uniform. He had decided to ask Andrew for a match, but a Mexican transvestite, Maria la Hija de Jesús, stopped him. She was wearing a turquoise gown that wrapped and tied behind her neck. Costume jewelry was pinned to her turban, bodice, and gloved arms.

"Darling," said Maria la Hija. "Do you like dis, and dis, and dot?" She pointed to her necklaces, bracelets, and a few other things.

"No, you're wearing them all wrong." The High Fiber Man, gripping a briefcase between his legs, rearranged the jewelry. Maria squealed when he touched her throat.

"Shhh," said Andrew. "Someone is working on something that's very important." No one paid him a bit of attention.

He had abandoned the new language to work on another chapter. Now he was writing about the time a horse threw him and he escaped without injury.

The High Fiber Man and Maria la Hija sat opposite Andrew and discussed Maria's married lovers. She had four. The High Fiber Man said that he lived above romance. "What? You expect me to believe?" said Maria. "I am not the idiot around here." She glared at Andrew.

He was trying to remember the name of the horse that threw him and did not feel Maria's eyes, nor did he notice that Dr. Walter Wormser, the noted Jungian analyst, was carefully observing the goings-on in the park. Dr. Wormser, whose grey hair clung to his head like a cloud of smoke, was standing outside the park and wondering when he should make himself known to the regulars. His three-piece suit was wrinkled and stained, and his "brief case," a Mexican shoulder bag embroidered with plumed serpents, was hanging from his neck like a giant amulet. With a pair of binoculars he brought Andrew T. Andrews into sharp focus, but his attention was soon diverted by a new arrival.

Victor L. (for Lloyd) Russell, the composer, not to be confused with his brother Victor L. (for Lawrence) Russell, winner of the Nobel Prize in medicine, entered the park on the Seventh Avenue side and sat on a bench directly across from Cherokee. Andrew had never heard of the composer, but he had heard of the Nobel scientist. Dr. Wormser, an authority on the interpretation of fairy tales, had heard of neither.

Victor L., the composer, was always being mistaken for Victor L., the late physician whose mutating flu vaccine was being used the world over. While the Nobel brother had been rapidly achieving fame, the composer had been slowly sinking into obscurity. His compositions were hardly ever played anymore except on his own Walkman. He was plugged into it that afternoon.

"I'm listening to myself," he announced in a loud voice. "Somebody has to. It might as well be me. I can't remember what I sound like anyway, so I could be listening to just about anybody. That's what happens when you get to be ninety-eight."

He was wearing a fisherman's hat with mosquito netting hanging from the brim. Because of his fear of all flying insects, no flesh was left exposed. "Anything that bites or stings is always biting or stinging me." He was listening to his fifth symphony and did not realize that he was shouting. "My blood is sweet." His voice carried into the traffic. "That's why they bite me. That's why I'm all covered up. I can't stand to be eaten on. Drives me crazy."

While conducting his symphony with a pencil, pigeons fluttered about his feet, and three parakeets, refugees from the bird store on Bleecker, strutted with the pigeons. Victor L. changed his

14

conducting tempo abruptly, and the birds took off like a cadenza in a mad scene.

They flew directly over Andrew's head and barely missed him, but he didn't realize this. He was striving for the courage to write about the time his mother kissed him goodnight twice in one evening. He was pleased with Proustian overtones, so pleased that he paid no attention to C.C. Wake.

C.C. called himself the Earthquake Expert of Lower Manhattan. He was standing near the Christopher Street entrance and lecturing on the killer quake that hit Mexico City a few years ago. He thought it had happened yesterday. He thought that the tremor that awakened New York City had happened that morning, but that was years ago also. C.C. believed he was a seismologist trained at Stanford. He didn't know exactly where Stanford was and sometimes confused it with Philadelphia. He came from Philadelphia. His family was Main Line, and for thirty years his mother paid him to stay away.

"I felt it hit before it hit," C.C. said. "That's how you can tell if it's a real quake. If you feel it one day and it hits the next day you can bet your life on it. Real quakes let you feel them beforehand. That goes for just about everything else too."

"What method will I use to break through to

15

this individual?" Dr. Wormser asked himself, while Andrew, chewing on his pencil, read a passage he had just written. He read aloud but only to himself. "In a consulting firm pregnant with resources I seemed to have been the only resource available. Flaming innuendos of discontent proved detrimental to my budding awareness. I found myself floundering with uncomfortable aspirations and drives." He was very pleased with this passage. It made him smile to read it.

Lulu, sometimes called the Statue Woman, strolled past Andrew as he chewed his eraser. At the narrow end of the park she turned a trashcan upside down and stood on it. She was a young woman with a sad face who shopped at the Salvation Army and lived on welfare.

"At last she has arrived," exclaimed Dr. Wormser, rapidly adjusting his spy glasses. He had been observing Lulu for months and was anxious to know her.

"Today I have a patriotic pose for you," she announced from the top of the trashcan. "I'll hold it exactly one hour, which I will time by counting 3,600 seconds."

The patriotic pose was very simple. Her right hand was protecting her heart. Her left hand was resting on her left shoulder.

"The erotic poses are your best," declared the High Fiber Man. "Do one."

"Oh yes, yes, yes," said **Dr.** Wormser with uncurbed exuberance.

"The erotic poses were part of yesterday's theme," the Statue Woman explained to the High Fiber Man. "Don't make me repeat myself, I'll get embarrassed. You'll make me turn red, and then I'll lose count. You know how I get. You know how confusing it is. I've already lost several seconds because of you." Suspiciously looking over her shoulder, she began whispering audibly. "The police don't want me here. They're timing me. They know how to count too."

Andrew had just written another sentence that pleased him. As the Statue Woman counted aloud, he read to himself.

"Assertive, perceptive, resonate voiced, I was held captive not only by a job description limited in nature, but also by an authority bold in participation, sympathetic in understanding, and allegorically equalistic in concern."

Just outside the park a large woman in a powder-blue gown was getting ready to sing an aria. Once on the brink of a promising career as a coloratura soprano, she had been forced to give up her ambition when a stage accident rendered her slightly tone deaf. "I no longer care to sing in the fine opera houses of the world," she explained to the small crowd waiting for her to begin. "My audience is right here on the streets."

17

"Do a mad scene," the High Fiber Man requested.

"Which one?" the soprano asked.

"Just any one as long as it's wild," the cereal heir joked.

The soprano turned on her cassette. "First I will sing 'Sempre libera'," she announced with hands folded at her expansive waistline. "You understand this is merely a warmup for today's speciality, the Queen of the Night."

Nearby, a woman dressed entirely in black was feeding the pigeons and starving the stray parakeets. "Those damn parakeets eat too much," she told Dr. Wormser as he crossed the street to enter the park.

"Who do those displaced parakeets represent to you?" he asked the woman, a noted book reviewer whose name was Frances Judd.

"Guess what's wrong with me?" she shouted in response to Dr. Wormser's question. He drew a blank as the soprano trilled into the heavy traffic. "I'll tell you what's wrong with me," said Frances, "I've read too many books, that's what. Thirty-seven a week is my quota. That's a little over five a day. Ask me something. See if I know what you're talking about."

"Nobody wants to ask you anything!" Cherokee Rose threw her voice across the park. She hated the reviewer. She hated all reviewers, but Andrew

18

liked them. He enjoyed imagining that the critics would one day praise his style as well as his content. He enjoyed knowing that one day everyone would be reading his many books and that college students would spend semesters analyzing his symbols and layers of meaning.

He quickly scanned his afternoon's work. "Well, I have stated it all." He gave himself a congratulatory pat on the leg. "Today I have written with uncontrollable insight." Then he got up to leave. No one noticed his exit except Dr. Wormser, who had just read a colleague's book, *The Once and Future Self.*

"I wonder if that man knows the difference between his once self and his future self," Dr. Wormser said, taking a seat next to the old composer.

"I wonder if anyone does," answered the High Fiber Man.

Victor L. Russell, thinking he had been greeted, nodded his head toward Dr. Wormser and went on conducting.

In the middle of Grove Street Andrew T. Andrews stopped and made a firm decision to work on his book another year. Then he reminded himself how lucky he was to have discovered Christopher Park. "That clean place at the end of the bench is my place," he assured himself.

"Nobody can bother me there. Those pigeons see to that."

He stood in the street and stared at the sky as if his next sentence were written on the clouds. Drivers were honking their horns and screaming for him to get out of the way, but Andrew was oblivious to the traffic jam he had caused.

Back in Christopher Park, C.C. Wake was lecturing on the Fourteenth Street fault. He was standing in front of Victor L. Russell, but the old composer wasn't listening. Still plugged into his Walkman, he was conducting the last movement of his fifth symphony while Dr. Wormser was introducing himself to Maria la Hija de Jesús.

"I could write volumes on your name alone," Dr. Wormser said, as though reciting a love verse.

"Who are you anyway?" asked Maria.

"I have two specialties," Dr. Wormser replied. "Personality assessment through tree drawings is one, and the other is the psychological interpretation of fairy tales. Have you ever read Cinderella?"

"Of course!" Maria said, insulted by the question as well as the familiarity in the doctor's voice.

"But do you understand that this innocent little story carries an often-neglected message for children as well as adults such as yourself?" Dr. Wormser asked.

"Leave me alone," Maria said.

20

"What the story tends to do," continued Dr. Wormser "is sooth a child's unconscious anxieties regarding sex and marriage. If, for example, the slipper represents the vagina and Cinderella's narrow foot represents her desire for penetration, then by taking the slipper and slipping her foot into it Cinderella is assuring the prince that she does not wish to castrate him. What she is saying on a symbolic level is that her parts will fit his parts, and his parts will fit her parts as though custom made."

"This is not the version of Cinderella I intend to tell my children," Maria de Jesús shrieked.

"Your parts aren't custom made for children," said the High Fiber Man. "We know who you are under that fancy dress."

"Let's get back to the point," said Dr. Wormser, his hair standing on end. "Cinderella and the prince are made for each other. This is what you must understand. The prince accepts Cinderella's vagina in the form of a slipper, and at the same time he approves of her desire to be plucked, symbolized by her beautiful little foot which slips in and out of the slipper."

"This is preposterous!" said Maria la Hija de Jesús.

"Give me your shoe," said Dr. Wormser. "I'll perform a little demonstration."

"Oh, be quiet," said the Statue Woman. "I'll

lose count if you don't." She had already reached her 2,359th second.

"I'll finish this novel by next spring," Andrew said, still standing in the middle of Grove Street. "That's only a year away. Then I'll write about something else." He inched his way across the street, and when he stepped onto the curb, the traffic started moving again. But at the next corner Andrew, without thinking, crossed Seventh Avenue South against the light. In the middle of the avenue three prepositional phrases popped into his head. Each described his main character: a man of jocular humor, of inconspicuous subtlety, and of perceptive intuitiveness. He stopped to write the phrases in his notebook while cab drivers blew their horns and shouted for him to move, and a flock of pigeons flew low over his head. Closing his notebook he continued on his way, without realizing that he had again halted the flow of traffic.

Across the street in Christopher Park, Dr. Wormser was holding up one of Maria's high-heeled shoes. "This is not a slipper," he said, pointing to the shoe. "This is a vagina!"

"You have never seen a vagina in your life," argued Maria la Hija.

"Yes he has," said Cherokee Rose. "His daughter Wickie Wormser is in my writing class."

"Please give me your foot," Dr. Wormser pleaded.

Reluctantly, Maria sat down and extended her right leg. While Dr. Wormser, assuming the role of the prince, ceremoniously knelt with Maria's shoe in hand, the book reviewer threw some breadcrumbs to a pigeon that had taken Andrew's place on the clean end of the bench. Within seconds the bench was filled with birds fighting to be fed.

"In and out, in and out, slips the foot into the slipper," sang Dr. Wormser. "Now what does this remind you of, anything in particular?"

"My shoe is not a vagina!" stated Maria la Hija.

"Yours may not be, but mine is!" shouted the High Fiber Man.

The soprano stopped singing. Mr. Russell stopped conducting. The Statue Woman broke her pose, and the High Fiber Man, along with Cherokee Rose, left the park quickly. Everyone else stared at Dr. Wormser. Still on his knees, he was caressing Maria's slipper.

"What a deviate," said the soprano. Turning her back on the scene, she hurled herself into the Queen of the Night's second aria, which startled the pigeons. All at once they flew away, leaving Andrew's place badly soiled.

"Pigeon droppings, pigeon droppings," said the

book reviewer, as though reciting an incantation. "This bench will never come clean."

On the far side of Seventh Avenue South, Andrew T. Andrews was suddenly gripped with the fear of becoming a complete failure. "What will happen if one day I can't think of anything else to write about?" he asked himself. "What if I run out of subject matter? What will I do then?"

He continued, somewhat reluctantly, on his way. His steps were slow and hesitant, but his mind was racing. Suddenly the feeling of having lost something swept over him. His notebook was in one hand and his now dull pencils in the other; a dollar bill along with his apartment keys were in one pocket but the other was empty. "This is all I started out with," he assured himself, yet the empty pocket haunted him. He walked on a little further. One leg felt heavier than the other, and that bothered him. "I feel out of balance again," he said. The sense of loss followed him down the street and into his building. Once in his apartment he arranged his pencils on the kitchen counter. He placed his notebook next to the pencils, and next to them his keys and the wadded-up dollar bill. "This is all I started out with," he told himself again. And yet the feeling of having lost something would not leave him. "I've left something very important back in the park," he said. "I wish I knew what it was."

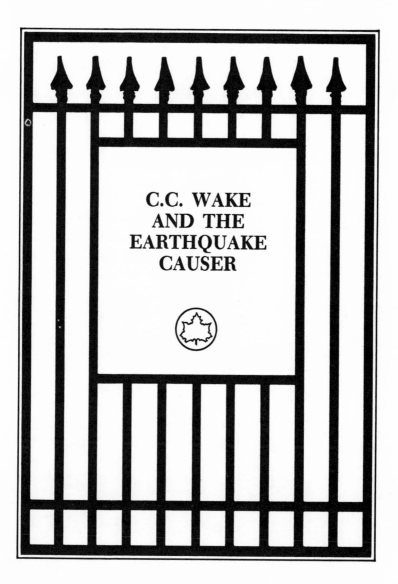

C.C. WAKE
AND THE
EARTHQUAKE
CAUSER

On a cool spring afternoon Cameo Miller, married to her ninth husband, sat in Christopher Park and wondered what would have happened to her had she not been the marrying type. Because Cameo was the walking image of her namesake, she had never had trouble attracting rich husbands. She had the face and figure of a Botticelli but was self-conscious of her appearance. People stared at her wherever she went. She had stopped traffic on the Champs Elysées, on Fifth Avenue, Rodeo Drive, and all the other great thoroughfares of the world. It was a burden to be so beautiful, and sometimes she found herself wishing that she looked like an ordinary person. Then she would be able to blend into any crowd. No one would stare at her, and she would never again feel angry, jealous, or lascivious eyes ripping her apart on every corner.

Wherever she went it was the same. Men grew weak in their knees when they saw her coming. Others claimed that the earth shook when she entered a room. Admirers all over the world had waited for her in hotel lobbies and had forced flowers, love letters, and boxes of candy into her arms. Women, on the other hand, had often spat on her from passing buses. They had shouted insults to her on the streets, and had clung ferociously to their husbands in Cameo's presence.

"I have never known what it's like to be just an average person," she said while sitting in the park and contemplating her unhappy present and uncertain future. "I have never known one calm day in my life."

The trees in Christopher Park had just begun to green, and Cameo, wrapped in crystal fox, was sipping coffee from a paper cup while trying to determine exactly what was wrong with her marriage. She had surrounded herself with no smoking signs in five languages and didn't want to be disturbed while attempting to analyze the dissatisfaction that had seeped into her life. "I am usually discontented this time of year," she confessed aloud while chewing on the paper cup. "That's why I've always met, married, or divorced my husbands during the spring.

Cameo and her current husband, Richard, lived in Houston, but they came to New York once a month on business. While Richard met with his clients, Cameo would wander around the city stopping traffic and feeling out of place. On one of their trips to Manhattan, Cameo had discovered Christopher Park. By then she had been around the world many times and had lived in many fashionable houses and cities, but the only place that felt comfortable was this little triangle near Sheridan Square. There she could almost relax. She could almost calm her rattled mind to the point of being able to plan her next move. "I am ready for a move," she said, staring into her coffee as if to divine the answers to her current predicament. A move to Cameo usually meant a new husband as well as a new address, but this time she was confused. She wasn't sure what she wanted or what she needed and that was why she was spending the afternoon in Christopher Park.

"I can't think at home anymore," she said to C.C. Wake, the Earthquake Expert of Lower Manhattan. "I don't have any trouble thinking in this park though."

"You can think here because we don't care what you're thinking about," C.C. replied. "If we cared what you were thinking about, you wouldn't be able to think here."

C.C. was sixty-five years old. He was thin and wrinkled. His white hair was cut short. A seersucker suit, his warm-weather uniform, was covered with a clear plastic raincoat in case of unexpected precipitation or a sudden drop in temperature. It had been an unpredictable spring.

C.C. had observed Cameo many times and had already figured out what was inside her mind, at least he thought he had. "I know who you are," he told her. "You're not famous to anybody but me."

"I've always wanted somebody to tell me who I really am and what I'm all about." Cameo wrapped the sleeves of her coat around her, bracing herself against a chilly gust of wind. "Who do you think I am? You seem to know."

"You're an earthquake causer," answered C.C. "I spotted you the first time you came here. I felt you too. When you walk you make the ground vibrate more than it naturally does. When you swing your hips to the right the earth swings to the left, and when you swing your hips to the left the earth swings to the right. Men are especially susceptible to this kind of ground motion. And the more money they've got the more you're able to make them shake. You can't make me shake though, and I've got money too. That proves how strong I am. I've got money, and I'm not shaking. See." He held out a steady hand.

For a moment Cameo was stunned. "I have been accused of opportunism," she said, thinking about her previous husbands whose names had escaped her at the moment.

"You have been accused of rocking solid foundations," C.C. informed her. "Anybody can look

30

at you and figure that out. There are many ways to make the earth shake, and your way is the most dangerous one to men."

"Is there any hope for me?" Cameo buried her face into the collar of her crystal fox.

"Hope?" exclaimed C.C. "There's always hope if hope is what you want, but I think you want more than hope. I think you're confusing *hope* with *help*. And if that's the case you're talking to one of the few people in the world who can help you. I just so happen to be an earthquake studier, and my speciality is earthquake causers such as yourself. Right now I don't know how to help you because I haven't studied you enough. That's why I'm going to go on studying you and studying you until I find out what I need to know."

"Oh, I've always believed in education," Cameo replied, as if defending herself.

"And I've always believed in questions." C.C. Wake spoke emphatically. "A question is the most wonderful thing when you come to think about it. And now here's one for you: I know you can make the earth shake, but can you feel it shaking too? That's what I'd like to know."

"I have felt the earth quiver," answered Cameo. "That's the truth. I have. Everywhere I go I feel like I'm walking on quicksand."

"They all say *quicksand!*" C.C. shouted.

"Quicksand turns up in every causer I've ever talked to."

"People turn and stare at me as though I've done something to them," Cameo continued in a low voice. She was folding her paper cup into a little square.

"Then you can cause the quakes and you can feel the quakes you cause." C.C. took this information and mulled it over. "This is something that we didn't know before today. This is something that's going to get written about."

He gave her a ticket stub with a phone number written on it. "I've got to go to my office now," he said, slowly coming to his feet. "But you can call me between one and three if it's not raining."

He walked to the main entrance and sat down on another bench just outside the gate. Soon a pay telephone, within easy reach, started ringing. C.C. answered it without leaving his seat. "Earthquake Headquarters. C.C. Wake speaking. Do you feel a quake coming on?"

Cameo stuffed her no-smoking signs into a Spanish leather shoulder bag and stood up slowly. Hoping that she was not drawing attention to herself, she tiptoed across the park. Under the wrought iron arch that framed the main entrance she stood perfectly still and watched C.C. Wake. A taxi driver honked his horn and whistled. "Get in lady, and let me make you feel good," he said in a seductive voice.

Embarrassed by the attention, Cameo made a mad dash to C.C.'s office bench and sat down beside him. In his presence she felt as though no one would notice her. Unlike her husbands, C.C. did not attempt to put her on display. He was patient and very calm, especially when talking on the telephone. She felt safe with him.

"I've got an earthquake causer sitting right here next to me, and I'm not one bit afraid," he told Dorothy Johnson who phoned once a week from North Carolina. Dorothy had been married many times, and, like Cameo, she saw herself as the victim of raving beauty.

"I never wanted to look like this," Dorothy told C.C.

"I've noticed one thing," C.C. explained. "The better looking you are, the more you're able to cause the earth to shake. The world is full of earthquake causers, and not all of them are women either. Lots of men call me at this number. They can be causers too. I know because I used to be one. Before I was a studier, I caused sidewalks to crack wide open. So you see, the goal of every causer is to become a studier. That way you won't hurt anybody."

C.C. handed the telephone to Cameo. "You

33

better talk to this one, because she's got your problem. You're not as rare as you might think."

"I'm not?" Cameo took the telephone while C.C. adjusted the buckles on his Birkinstock sandals. He wore them with heavy socks.

"People stare at me too," Cameo told Dorothy Johnson. "Now be calm, and take some deep breaths. Pretty soon you'll stop shaking, and you'll be able to go back to the grocery store and look for your purse. I'm sure it's still there. Nobody is staring at you because they hate you, they just hate what you represent . . ."

"Earth shakers are hard to be around unless you once were one," C.C. said to a passing policeman. "If they don't get help, they'll eventually cause the world to split apart. That's why we have experts in the field."

"How many calls have you taken today?" asked the policeman.

"One call and one visit," answered C.C. "Your cousin in Nebraska, he called again yesterday. He's getting to be more of a studier than a causer. He's about to graduate is what I mean, and I don't have time for graduates. Right now I've got two causers on the same line. This is something new I'm trying for the first time, and it's working too."

The policeman tipped his hat and walked on. He had been on this beat for years. Sometimes

34

he would walk over to Washington Square or the Bowery and find someone who needed a sympathetic ear. Then he would give the person a quarter and C.C.'s office number. "Call between one and three o'clock if it's not raining," he would say. "Just ask for C.C. Wake the Earthquake Expert. He specializes in anything that's shaking you up."

Gradually C.C.'s reputation as a street psychologist became well known in many parts of the country. "I receive calls from all over Manhattan, the United States, and the world," he told Cameo when she hung up the phone. "Everybody's got a problem and everybody's problem can be linked up in some way to ground motion. If we didn't have so many problems we wouldn't have what I call Earthquake Sickness. It's pretty bad stuff, but it's curable. I can attest to that."

The Seventh Avenue subway, passing under the park, made the sidewalk vibrate. "Brace yourself!" C.C. shouted. "Somebody's gone out of control."

Cameo held on to the bench and C.C.'s arm.

After the subway passed and the sidewalk stopped quivering, C.C. placed both hands over his heart. "That was a close call," he sighed. "So far we've never had a major quake, and that's a miraculous record, considering all the causers we've got in this part of the world. We've got twelve causers to one studier. Don't ask me how I know."

He looked at his watches. He was wearing three on his left arm. "This first watch is New York time," he informed Cameo. "The second one is Midwest time. And the third one is Los Angeles time." On the other arm he was wearing only two watches. "This one," he explained, pointing to the first watch, "is London, England time, and this one is no-time. I keep one no-time watch just in case someone calls me from a time zone I haven't spoken to before. That could happen you know."

"Does it help you to know what time of day the causer is calling from?" Cameo asked.

"Not only that," C.C. said. "I like to be able to look at my watches and say: 'It's seven o'clock down in Oklahoma City and ole Charlotte Weisenbaker's getting ready to go to work.' She's a civil servant and has headaches so bad the ground starts bubbling up under her feet. So every morning at seven I just think about her a little while. She knows I do, and that makes her feel better. Her son lives somewhere over there." He pointed across Seventh Avenue South. "Bedford Street, I think it is. Well, he put her up to calling me. He said she's a nervous wreck, but I think he's talking about himself without knowing it."

C.C. pointed to his second watch. "I know four people living in this time zone," he said.

"Now you know five," Cameo told him. "When I go back home I'll call you every day. We'll talk."

"If it's not raining," C.C. reminded her.

"If it's not raining." Cameo got up to leave, but C.C. stopped her.

"Let me show you my place," he said. "I don't live far from here."

They walked west along Christopher Street and then turned right onto Bleecker. "You're a causer and you know how to talk to causers," C.C. said as they walked along. Almost everybody they passed spoke to him, including the children. "You've helped me learn a very important thing today. Causers can be helpers before they become studiers."

For a moment they stopped at the exotic bird store. "I've got a friend living here." C.C. pointed to a cage hanging from the ceiling. "That parrot right there. He bites everybody but me, and that's why nobody will buy him. Nobody will pay him a bit of attention. It's a terrible thing when nobody pays attention to you." C.C. waved to the bird.

"It's worse," Cameo said, "when everybody pays you the wrong kind of attention."

"Surely not *everybody*," C.C. said. "That's a

37

lot of people. Do you know how many people *everybody* includes?"

"Okay, I get your point," Cameo said, embarrassed by her self-involvement. Across the street someone whistled at her. She refused to turn her head.

"Hey, are you for real?" the whistler yelled. Cameo became tense. She took C.C. by the arm and forced him to walk a little faster.

"The wrong kind of thinking," said C.C. "draws the wrong kind of attention. Just think about it. You'll see that I'm right."

They settled into a more agreeable pace as they crossed Abingdon Square on their way to Jane Street. Occasionally Cameo looked back to make sure no one was following them.

"You have nothing to worry about," C.C. assured her. "Nobody's looking at you. Everybody's got better things to do. Besides, we're almost there."

C.C. lived in the Jane West Hotel. His room faced the Hudson River, and he was proud of his view. "Millionaires pay a lot to see what I see," he told Cameo when he unlocked his door.

The Jane West was a transient hotel, but there were a few permanent residents, and C.C. was one of them. He had lived there almost forty years. His room smelled of candle wax, cloves, and oranges. A bookcase filled with incomplete sets of encyclopedias divided the room, and the walls were covered with picture postcards and letters. All the messages were similar.

" 'Dear Mr. Wake, After I talk to you I feel so much better.' " Cameo read the message aloud. " 'One day I hope we can meet. Give my nephew a big hello. Tell him to stop and think while he's in the big city. Virginia Martin. April 4, 1984.' "

Cameo read from another card, postmarked Baltimore, 1979. " 'I think I'm turning into a studier now. Thanks to you I don't feel so shaky on my feet. Wendell Palmer.' "

" 'Dear C.C., My sister in Detroit will call you. She has the same problem I have. We just can't sit still. Please talk to her the same way you talked to me.' "

Cameo wandered around the room, reading some of the cards and glancing at others. "How many of these people have you met?" she asked.

"Not many," C.C. answered. He turned on his hot plate to make coffee. "Earthquake causers often stay in one place. You're the exception."

While waiting for the water to boil, C.C. washed his best cups, and Cameo continued to wander around the room. It was very tidy and thoughtfully arranged. An overstuffed chair faced the window, and a gate-leg table with a reading lamp on top of it had been placed near the chair. On the other side of the bookcase a small waterbed was partially covered with a blue blanket.

Cameo sat on the easychair and stared out the window at the Hudson. C.C. was still washing his cups. He had not had company in a long time and wanted to make a good impression. Projecting the right image was suddenly very important to him, and for the first time in months, possibly a year, he thought about his family. Only his brothers were left. He wondered if appearances were still very important to them, also.

"I'm going to tell you something about me you don't know," said C.C. "I'm Main Line."

"Main Line?" Cameo asked with a puzzled look.

"Main Line Philadelphia," C.C. said. "I've got four brothers; two doctors and two lawyers, but I'm the outcast. I didn't have their interests is what I mean. When I was a boy all I wanted to do was watch demolition men breaking up sidewalks and streets. Then I'd go study the cracks they made to find out if they meant anything, which of course they did. I was able to figure out that the cracks foretold man-made disasters of all kinds, especially those affecting the balance of the earth on its axis. That's when I got me a sledge hammer and started cracking up sidewalks all by myself. But this kind of behavior wasn't accepted back then, and I was forced to work at night so no one would see me. I took rubbings of the cracks I made so I could study them the next day in my room."

"What did you learn?" asked Cameo.

"I learned how much pressure it takes to break things apart," he said while spooning once-used coffee grounds into his drip pot. "Now I don't need to do much studying any more, because I developed what it takes to feel somebody's ground motion. I feel it every time somebody has a crack-up or gets the shakes. I can feel it even in my sleep."

He walked over to the waterbed and lifted the blue blanket. The mattress was only half filled with water. "Never use more water than this," he explained. "If you do, you'll feel the big quakes, but not the little ones. The little ones are sometimes more important than the big ones. That's what the books will tell you. Every time I feel the slightest quiver, no matter what time of night it is, I get up and look at the map. I try to figure out if it's somebody I know who's causing the shake-up."

"How did you learn all this," Cameo asked, sinking into her crystal fox.

"I went to lots of schools, including my own," C.C. told her. "I can't remember all the names. Some of them were outside schools, some were inside schools. From the time I was thirteen, I was in special schools of one kind or another. I've been tested with wires strapped to my head too, and after that I became more susceptible to ground motion than ever before."

"And after that?" Cameo asked.

"After that came another round of special schools, and special institutions, and special testing places, and after a few years no one had to ask where I was anymore because everyone already knew I was someplace *special*. Some place where people like me need to be, right here at the Jane West."

Cameo watched C.C. pouring weak coffee into a spotless cup he had chosen for her.

"I tell you something else that I know that most people don't know that I know," C.C. said, handing her the cup handle first. "Most of the people who call me are talking about one thing, and I'm talking about something else, but I don't see that that makes too much difference in this day and time. Anybody who feels a quake coming on is in serious trouble whether they take it seriously or not. So this is what I tell them: 'If you don't make the earth shake, the earth won't make you shake.' In the end they always tell me I'm right. They always come around to my kind of thinking. I stay with them until they do."

"And then they send you all these cards of thanks," said Cameo, glancing around the room.

"Not only that," said C.C. "they send me checks to help keep the headquarters going. I tell them to save me the trouble by making their checks out to me, C.C. Wake, and then send them, deposit only, directly to the Chase Manhattan bank. Everybody knows me there."

"You must have a lot of money," said Cameo.

"I've got over $75,000," C.C. told her. "Most of that money comes from quake causers who have gone on to become quake studiers."

"That's quite a lot of money," Cameo exclaimed. "What are you going to do with it?"

"What *can* I do with it?" C.C. poured milk into his coffee. "I enjoy knowing the money is there because in the case of sickness I might need some of it, but otherwise it's not good for a thing. Money can't cure a problem like yours, for example."

"Believe me, I've found that out the hard way." Cameo stared into her cup.

"Then you should stick around here," C.C. said, sugaring his coffee heavily as he spoke. "You'd learn a lot."

"Are there rooms?" Cameo asked.

"Plenty," answered C.C. He drank his coffee in three giant swallows. Cameo watched him.

"I just can't stand to think about that telephone ringing on rainy days with no one responsible out there to answer it," she said, staring into C.C.'s

43

eyes. "If you don't mind, I'd like to take the rainy-day shift. I've got a good umbrella."

"You've also got a sensible way about you," C.C. said. "You know how to listen when you're supposed to listen and how to talk when you're supposed to talk."

"Then is it a deal?" asked Cameo.

"You've got yourself a business partner," C.C. assured her. "It relieves my mind to make this important decision. Listening to all these earthquake problems isn't easy, you know, especially this time of year. For some reason or other spring is my busy season. There are days when I receive so many calls I feel like I could start cracking all over again. And then there's the larger concern. He paused before going on. "Somebody needs to take my place when I'm not around anymore. I've been thinking about that a lot."

They shook hands to close their business agreement. "I'm about to change the way I live and the way I think," Cameo said. "And I'm not going to get married again to do it. This is new for me."

Out on the Hudson the QE II, its decks filled with passengers, was gliding down the river toward the ocean. For a moment Cameo wanted to be on it. For a moment her heart skipped a beat. Then she sipped her coffee and planted both feet firmly on the floor. C.C. Wake opened his notebook and started recording everything that had happened to him that day, and Cameo stared at the passenger ship until it was no longer framed by the hotel window. Suddenly, she had the sensation of movement. It seemed as though the Jane West Hotel was floating along at a leisurely pace while the rest of the world was shaking.

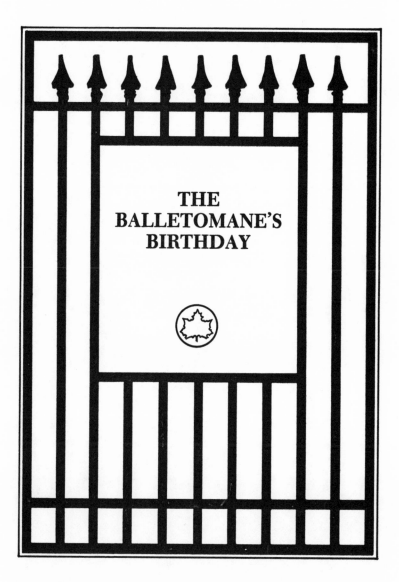

THE
BALLETOMANE'S
BIRTHDAY

Shelley was determined to celebrate her for-
tieth birthday by dancing the *Wili* Hop. She
called it the *Wili* Hop. No one else did. *Giselle*
was not Shelley's favorite ballet, but the *Wili* Hop
in the second act always thrilled her, even when
it was danced badly. "To see those girls hopping
toward each other, and through each other, and
back through each other does my heart good,"
she told her friend Charles Maplewood, who had
agreed to give her a birthday party. "Please invite
lots of people who will cooperate."

"I can't invite very many," Charles, a baritone
at the Metropolitan Opera, explained, "because
Lulu has come home."

Lulu was his upstairs neighbor. Her real name
was Judy, but everyone called her Lulu because
it seemed to fit. She was twenty something and
had never been well mentally. Once she started
screaming out the window, only the police could
silence her. The precinct always sent its most
handsome officers to walk her around the block

49

or take her for coffee. Then, for a day or two, she'd be calm again.

"She's just been released from Bellevue," Charles told Shelley. "And besides that, she's approaching the anniversary of her ex-lover's marriage. That's always a difficult time for her, and the only reason why I'm sorry to be giving a party. Noise sets her off."

Charles narrowed the invitation list down to three, including Shelley and himself. He insisted that he could invite no more, and Shelley was furious about that. But what could she do? She had her heart set on dancing the *Wili* Hop, and nothing would stop her now, even if she had to dance it alone.

Guillermo Garcia, who was accustomed to Shelley's ongoing bouts of dance fever, was the third on the list. Shelley and Charles had met Mo waiting on line for standing room. That night Gelsey was dancing the role of Giselle. Baryshnikov was partnering her, and Martine Van Hamel was dancing the Queen of the *Wilis*.

"I have always understood that *Giselle* is a two-ballerina ballet," Shelley said as they queued up at six a.m. "There are many fine Giselles dancing about. But a good *Wili* queen is hard to come by. Van Hamel is perfect in my opinion."

To the man standing in front of her she said,

"I hope you know we're in for a real treat tonight. We just might see history too."

That man was Guillermo, and at the time he was employed as a hair stylist in an all-night salon on St. Marks Place. Because he had been born in Mexico City, Shelley was forever asking him why Mexico hadn't produced great ballerinas like Oklahoma. She had been born in Oklahoma, and she would not let anyone forget it. Maria and Marjorie Tallchief came from there. So did Yvonne Chouteau and Moscelyne Larkin. Rosella Hightower was born in Ardmore, Shelley's home town. She was always spouting the names of Oklahoma's Indian ballerinas as though everyone was personally acquainted with them.

"If you want to become a classical ballerina, you must arrange to be born in Oklahoma." That was her advice to young dancers at the American Ballet Academy where she worked as a secretary. "Indian blood seemed to help too. Probably because dance is the first and most primitive of the arts. When man cannot express in words his innermost feelings, he turns to movement. He either moves himself or persuades others to move for him. My shrink, Dr. Walter Wormser, told me this, and I have found it to be the key to unlocking myself as well as others."

✿

On the day of Shelley's birthday party Charles

was standing in Capezio's waiting to be waited on. Finally a young man with quite a turnout offered to help him.

"I'd like to buy three practice tutus," Charles said. "Romantic length, like Giselle."

The clerk disappeared behind a curtain, and presently returned with three paper tubes. The tutus were inside them.

"Here are your tutus, sir."

"Thank you," Charles replied. "I intend to wear all three at once."

"Oh good," the sales clerk exclaimed. "They stack beautifully."

"I wonder how many times a day he gets to say that," Charles remarked to himself as he left the shop.

At seven o'clock Mo was the first to arrive. His cat, Miss Farrell, sometimes called Suzanne, was draped around his neck. Miss Farrell was black with white feet and enjoyed being lifted.

Charles gave Mo one of the long white tutus, and Mo put it on his head.

"Do you think Miss Shelley will approve?" he asked. Miss Farrell disappeared into the kitchen.

"No!" Charles answered. "You know how she is. Ballet is very serious business to her. Tutus are not meant to be worn on the head. She'll tell you."

Both Charles and Mo were wearing white

sweatpants, t-shirts, and socks. Charles stepped into his tutu and pulled it up to his waist, but Mo refused to conform.

At seven-thirty Shelley arrived. Charles opened the door and she just stood there. Usually she came rushing into the apartment, but not tonight. Charles sensed that something was troubling her. He thought it might be her age. She continued to stand there without speaking. Her hair was in a bun, and her face was powdered white. She didn't look forty. Live placenta had discouraged the wrinkles. She told everyone she was thirty and got away with it.

Finally Charles broke the silence. "Happy birthday," he said with a big smile.

"Charles!" Shelley pronounced his name as if out of breath. "Are you depressed? Tell me the truth. If you lie to me I'll find out about it."

Shelley had gone through ten years of Jungian analysis and to her everything was either depressing, symbolic, or mythological.

"No, I'm not depressed." Charles answered sharply.

"Well you're about to be," she informed her host. "You're about to be so depressed you won't know what to do. When I tell you what I have just found out, you're going to be sick for the rest of the night, so just get ready." She shook her pointe shoes in Charles's face.

"There's trouble in paradise," she continued. "Blue Eye Shadow is back."

Blue Eye Shadow was Shelley's name for a male dancer she had never admired in any way. Two seasons ago when he retired, Shelley threw a party to celebrate the occasion. Now he had returned.

"He's not a bad dancer," Charles said, "but you're right about the eye shadow. No one should wear that much, not even a ballerina."

"I am SICK over this!" Shelley said, beating her toeshoes against the doorfacing. "I'm softening these shoes and releasing my anger all at once," she explained. "I don't have time to waste."

"I was hoping you wouldn't find out about Blue Eye Shadow until after your party," Charles confessed.

"If they think I'm going to spend good money to look at that painted face, they're crazy." Shelley still stood in the hall. "They'll have to sell valium with the tickets to get me there," she shouted. This is further proof of what I've been saying for the last five years: The Golden Age of Ballet is almost over. I keep telling you this, but you refuse to believe me, even though I've seen history."

"I can make it through his eye shadow," Charles said. "It's all that lip licking that bothers me. He can't dance without showing his tongue."

"That's because he has something to say and can't say it or doesn't know how to say it," Shelley lectured, leaning heavily on her ten years of analysis. "What's on the tip of his tongue is what I'd like to know? What does he want to spit out? What does he want to reveal and can't? The next time I see him, do you know what I'm going to do? I'm going to give him the name of a good analyst. Mine. Dr. Wormser has done me the world of good. I wouldn't be standing here today if it weren't for him. With his help I've released all my pent-up anger and resentment."

"Released it or become more aware of it?" asked Charles.

"I said released, and I meant released!" Shelley's voice was on edge.

Mrs. Grimes, Charles's next-door neighbor, had come to her door and was looking at them disapprovingly, Charles in particular. Shelley stopped ranting and looked at Mrs. Grimes, who was staring at Charles.

"I think it's the tutu," Shelley whispered to her friend. "You better let me come in." She leaped into the apartment as Charles said good night to his neighbor.

Once inside the apartment Shelley's mood changed.

"Oh, listen to that music," she said, touching her ear.

55

It was the second act of *Giselle*. Mo turned up the volume, and Shelley danced down the hall on her way to becoming a *Wili*.

Mo embraced her with the tutu on his head, but she did not embrace back. "Ballet is serious business," she said. "Tutus are not meant to be worn on the head. You look like a bride, and you can't be a bride. Not if you're a *Wili*. May I remind you that a *Wili* is the spirit of a young girl who has died tragically and unnecessarily and all because of the man she loves and never gets to marry. Please refer to your program notes if you don't believe me."

Shelley had twenty years of ballet programs under her bed and thought that everybody else did too. Autographed toe shoes covered her apartment walls, and there was hardly a dancer she hadn't met. She started going to the ballet when she was an exchange student in Vienna. Since then she had hopped around the world for one purpose: to see every major ballet company in existence. She kept abreast of all company gossip and promotions. She knew who was dancing what and when. She could reel off the names of the Soviet dancers with an impeccable accent and claimed to be fluent in French. Only Charles knew that her facility was limited to the correct pronunciation of ballet terms and the practiced skill of counting rapidly to thirty-two.

"I have seen ballet history," she reminded Mo, as if he had forgotten. "But I have never seen a tutu anywhere but where a tutu belongs, and that's around the waist. Someone correct me if I'm wrong."

"Why would we want to correct someone who's seen history?" Mo asked.

"No one would dare," Charles said.

The music swelled. Charles turned down the volume for fear of upsetting Lulu. Mo moved his tutu to its proper place, and Shelley slipped on her new pointe shoes.

"Hurry, this is the best part," she said, pointing to the speaker nearest her. "The *Wili* Hop is about to begin. Take your places. Charles, we do need a fourth for this. How could you deprive us?"

"Miss Farrell will be the fourth," said Mo. With Suzanne in his arms, he stood on the opposite side of the room from Charles and Shelley.

"Now watch me carefully," Shelley demanded, balancing on one leg while extending the other behind her. "You must hold your upper body parallel to the floor." Her tone was very serious. "Extend one arm *a l'arriere* and extend the other *a l'avant.*

On the musical cue they hopped toward each other while attempting to hold this position.

57

"This is called *arabesque voyagé,*" Charles explained as he hopped past Mo.

"I thought it was called the *Wili* Hop." Mo was almost out of breath.

"That's exactly what it is," Shelley informed them. "There's no other name for it either, not tonight anyway."

They turned and repeated the hopping step in the opposite direction. They passed through each other again. And then it was over.

"The *Wili* Hop is so very brief," Shelley complained. "I always forget that. It seems to come and go before I've really enjoyed it."

Charles returned the needle, and they attempted to dance Shelley's favorite passage again, and then again, and yet again they somehow managed to hop across the room. Finally they fell exhausted onto the floor. Miss Farrell chose a soft chair.

"Libation," Shelley said after a brief rest. "We need to toast this occasion."

It was just what Mo had been waiting for. He uncorked the champagne. They lifted their glasses and spouted birthday wishes. Then Charles brought out the presents. Shelley opened Mo's first. She found a pair of worn-out tights which Mo had autographed himself in the name of Anthony Dowell.

"Anthony!" Shelley exclaimed, kissing the air

around her. She always did that when she said
his name. "I will never, never, never remove this
present." She tied the tights around her neck.

Next she opened Charles's present. It was a
video of *Giselle* and Shelley insisted on seeing
the second act at once.

While they watched the Queen of the *Wilis*
bourrée across the stage, Lulu decided to act up.
"No, I was not invited to his goddamn wedding,"
she screamed out her window to the early summer
crowd that had gathered in Christopher Park.
"But I went anyway, didn't I?"

"I believe that girl's depressed," Shelley announced as she ran to the open window. She
leaned out and looked up. Lulu was standing on
her third floor fire escape and striking erotic poses
to amuse the people in the park.

"When her boyfriend left her, she fell apart,
I mean completely," Charles said. "Now she goes
over to the park every afternoon to strike poses.
That's why we call her the Statue Woman."

"She behaves this way because she wants people to notice her." Shelley spoke with the voice
of an authority. "I learned this from my ten years
with Dr. Wormser. He used to have a patient
just like her."

"I wonder if her boyfriend was worth it?" Mo
asked.

"Have some respect," Shelley demanded. "That

girl's on her way to becoming a *Wili*. Ask me. I
know."

Shelley crawled through the kitchen window
and stood on the fire escape. Mo followed her.
"Don't get her more upset than she already is,"
Charles pleaded "You don't have to live here and
listen to her all night, but I do."

"Come down from there and let me talk to
you." Shelley raised her voice, and the people
in the park had no trouble hearing her. "I know
how you're suffering. Believe me I ought to know.
I've had five miserable marriages and lived to tell
about them. There's not one thing you can name
that I haven't lived through or thought about.
And I'm not bitter either."

"Then why is she shouting?" asked Mo.

"Because she's not bitter, of course," replied
Charles. Soon he was standing on the fire escape
with his two friends. Their tutus were touching.

Lulu's hair was half up and half down. Mascara
mixed with tears was running down her face. Her
lips quivered.

"God, I wonder if she ever thought about being
a ballerina?" Shelley whispered. "She looks more
like Giselle than Giselle."

"Don't invite her down here," Charles begged.
But it was too late.

"We're going to help you dance your troubles
away," Shelley whispered sympathetically. She

had gone up the fire escape to comfort Lulu. "But first I have to ask you a very important question. Have you ever been to the ballet? Now tell me the truth. I'll find out about it if you lie."

Lulu shook her head no.

"Oh good!" Shelley took Lulu by the hand and led her down the fire escape. "Ballet can change your life, and it will. It has certainly changed mine." She helped Lulu through the window and led her to the television set. "Just watch this." Shelley pointed to the picture. "You don't have to say a thing."

Martine Van Hamel was finishing her second act solo.

"Now, *she* is what you call a *Wili*." Shelley spoke with schoolteacher emphasis while Lulu stood mesmerized in front of the television. "She is the Queen of the *Wilis*. And in a few minutes all the other *Wilis* will be out there dancing what *we* called the *Wili* Hop."

"What *you* call the *Wili* Hop," Charles corrected.

"That's not really what it's called," added Mo.

"It most certainly is!" Shelley was ready to argue. "Don't interrupt me at a time like this."

"Oh look!" She pointed at the television with both hands. "Here come the *Wilis* in their long skirts and pale faces. Don't they look fresh from the grave?"

61

No one answered.

"*Giselle* is the story of love, betrayal, death, and posthumous revenge," Shelley lectured. Her eyes were glued to the screen. "*Wilis* are spirits of young virgins who have died of broken hearts. They come back to look for the men who did them wrong. And when they find them, they dance them to death and enjoy every minute of it too."

"That's what I'd like to do," said Lulu.

"Yes, and you should." Shelley stared directly into Lulu's eyes. "It would be very good for you."

"Thank you, Doctor." said Mo.

"Please be careful," Charles warned Shelley. He was squeezing Miss Farrell in his arms.

For a long time they watched Lulu watching the ballet. Then the gamekeeper appeared and the *Wilis* danced him to death. The queen was in her hour. She held branches above her head and issued commands. Lulu imitated her.

"Oh, I was mistaken," Shelley readily admitted. "At first I thought you were Giselle, but you're not. You're the Queen of the *Wilis*. And you are perfect, perfect, perfect for the role. Too bad you're not a ballerina."

She balled up Lulu's hair, and relinquished her own tutu. "These tutu's aren't full enough for a queen," she said with irritation. She forced her two friends to relinquish their tutus also. She put all three of them on Lulu.

"Oh look," Shelley exclaimed. "They stack beautifully."

"Who would have thought it," Charles said.

"Just what we need," Shelley informed him, "another *Wili* for the *Wili* Hop." She turned off the VCR and turned on the stereo. The volume was full blast. Shelley and Lulu on one side of the room started hopping toward Mo and Charles on the other. While Miss Farrell watched from the sofa, they hopped toward each other and past each other. Then they turned and did it again.

"Instant replay, si vous plait!" Shelley was in her glory.

The needle was returned, and they waited for their musical cue. Shelley waited in perfect fifth.

Over and over they danced the *Wili* Hop, now more for Lulu than Shelley. Lulu seemed to have entered another state of mind. She was calm, the way she was after New York City's Finest took her walking. Her eyes were glazed, and the sadness had left her face. Shelley, Charles, and Mo sat down with Miss Farrell and watched the new queen take the stage.

"She actually remembers some of the steps," said Mo. He could remember steps like nobody else, including Shelley, who envied his ability.

"Of course she can remember some of the

steps," said Shelley. "It's instinct. Inside every woman there's a *Wili.*"

Lulu was now carried away. She swung at Mo with her fists.

"She's trying to dance you to death," whispered Shelley. "Let her do it. She needs to."

Mo stood up, and Lulu danced him around the room.

"This is thrilling!" exclaimed Shelley.

"Somehow, I'd feel a lot more comfortable if you weren't enjoying it so much," Charles confessed.

When Mo collapsed in feigned exhaustion, Shelley said, "Why do I feel as though I've waited a whole lifetime for this?" Then Lulu danced down the hall and out the door, slamming it behind her.

"We must follow her." Shelley shouted to her friends as though they were blocks away. Mrs. Grimes opened her door to find out what was going on. Three figures darted through the corridor, and she slammed her door fast.

Out on the street Lulu was dancing a derelict to death. He fell against a street lamp, and Lulu laughed. Then, executing grands jetés followed by a series of *Wili* Hops, she danced across Grove Street and into the park.

Charles stopped running long enough to point a finger of accusation at Shelley. "You have created a monster!" he shouted. "What makes you think you have the answer to everybody's problems?"

"Because I do," Shelley replied with confidence.

They continued the chase through Christopher Park and along West Fourth Street to the Yellow Parrot Café, where Lulu danced for the benefit of the sidewalk diners. "This must be some kind of publicity stunt," someone commented as Shelley forced a path through the Saturday night crowd. By then Lulu had danced to the corner of West Fourth and Avenue of Americas. She looked both ways before she danced across the street.

"Her jetés are quite grand." Mo stopped to study her line. "She's almost flying."

"As if by the gods possessed!" exclaimed Shelley.

"We'll never catch up with her," Charles said, "God only knows where she's going."

"She'll be all right," Shelley assured her friends as Lulu disappeared into the night. "She's so inside herself she's beside herself. That's all."

"You're talking about yourself, aren't you?" asked Mo.

"No," Shelley answered seriously, "I'm just the opposite."

Shelley was still wearing the forged tights

around her neck and her pointe shoes on her feet. The ribbons were untied. Her white leotard was dirty, and her hair was falling out of its bun.

"I can't believe you're forty," Charles said.

"Don't tell anyone, Charles." Shelley spoke in her most threatening voice. "I'll call you a liar if you do. Besides, I don't ever intend to have another birthday."

"I was about to suggest that," Mo said, as the three of them, now a bit lonely without Lulu, walked arm in arm back to Sheridan Square. The evening was mild, and yet a faint trace of a heat wave that would soon engulf the city was hovering above their heads. At Christopher Park they decided to sit down and enjoy the good weather while it lasted.

"So Blue Eye Shadow is about to make a comeback," Mo said, as he wiped off a bench.

"I don't think we need to talk about him right now," Charles suggested.

"To be perfectly honest, I'm glad he's back," said Shelley. "When I introduce him to Lulu, he'll never dance again."

THE
HIGH FIBER MAN
AND THE LITTLE
PAINTED LADY

Since early afternoon the High Fiber Man, the thirty-four-year-old heir to a small rice cereal fortune, had been wandering through the Port Authority Bus Terminal in search of someone to kidnap. Dressed in a tuxedo and carrying a black briefcase, he had been watching young girls arrive and depart but had not been able to decide which one to force into his limousine. He had never kidnapped anyone before, and he was nervous, almost frightened, because of his lack of practical experience. "This is new to me," he kept reminding himself. "That's why I have to be careful."

Two young women had caught his fancy earlier in the day, but after following each of them through the Port Authority he had decided that neither would serve his purpose. At six-thirty in the evening, he was exhausted by the anxiety of his mission combined with a suffocating heat wave that had fallen over the city like an electric blanket. His tuxedo was damp and wrinkled. His black toupee was beginning to pucker, and his little round fingers were nervously fiddling with the handle on his briefcase. "One more bus," he kept saying to no one in particular. "Just one more."

The bus he was waiting for was coming from the South. Something told him that a southern girl was what he needed. Someone who wasn't wise to the ways of the city. Someone who still trusted people, even strangers.

The bus arrived fifteen minutes late. As the passengers exited, the High Fiber Man rejected each of them after careful scrutiny until at last he saw her, Ellen Smith, an eighteen-year-old from West Virginia who had come to the city to be discovered.

She was wearing a small-brimmed straw hat and her Sunday best, a navy-blue dress with large white polka dots and a ruffled neckline that plunged slightly. Her hair was red and so were her shoes, her lips, and her cheeks. False eyelashes partially covered her blue-green lids, which were lined in black all the way around. Face powder was still clinging to her shoulders. In spite of her heavy make-up her innocence came shining through. She had never been to New York City before, and to the High Fiber Man, it was obvious.

"Little Painted Lady," he said, taking her suitcase and ushering her through the crowd, "your limousine is waiting."

"But I can't afford a limousine," Ellen protested. Suddenly, the terminal's stale humidity left her queasy, and the exhaust fumes burned her eyes. "My father," she said, almost unable to speak, "only gave me enough money for a taxi."

"Your father hired me to meet you," the High Fiber Man said, guiding his carefully chosen victim through the waiting room and onto Eighth Avenue where his black limousine was parked. He opened the door, and gently forced Ellen into the back seat. "You must sit on the right," he told her. "That's the best side for seeing the city. Leave your suitcase on the left." Quickly, he memorized the placement of her suitcase, and the angle of her body on the seat as well as her traveling attire. Then he took the wheel.

"I'm going to the Barbizon Hotel," she said.

"I know," her driver answered. "But I've been hired to give you a short tour first." He took her for a spin through Times Square and the theatre district.

Ellen, breathless with excitement, read the marquees aloud. "I'm going to be the next Julie Harris," she informed her driver as she gazed reverently at the Shubert Theatre.

"When you're famous I'll tell everyone I was

71

the first to show you the town." The High Fiber Man was very nervous. His voice quivered. To calm himself down he decided to drive around a little longer than he had planned. Along the way he pointed out the sights: Carnegie Hall, the Plaza Hotel, St. Patrick's Cathedral. They circled Rockefeller Center and Saks Fifth Avenue, and then they sped past the Public Library, Lord and Taylor's, and the Empire State Building. Finally they came to the Washington Arch, marred with graffiti, four-letter words followed by names and phone numbers.

"It's just beautiful," Ellen exclaimed, leaning out the window to look at the arch. "I've only seen it in pictures."

"I'm going to take you someplace you'll like very much." The High Fiber Man smiled. He had regained his courage. "A friend of mine lives near here. You need to meet her."

In front of a dilapidated townhouse on Barrow Street he stopped the limousine. "Right over there is the Cherry Lane Theatre." He pointed to a small building. "And right here is a house where lots of important people used to live. One still does. I wonder if you'll recognize her." Briefcase in hand, he got out to open Ellen's door while she quickly inspected her make-up with a small hand mirror equipped with a light. The colors on her face had faded and that displeased her. "I must retouch my make-up," she said while the High Fiber Man stood impatiently on the curb. She repainted her lips and cheeks with a brilliant crimson, added sparkling eyeshadow to her lids, and dusted herself with an iridescent powder.

"My dear, you glow in the dark," said the High Fiber Man as Ellen, hanging onto her suitcase, slid out of the limousine. "No need to take your luggage," he added, speaking in a suspiciously kind voice. "It's safe in the car. Besides, we'll only be here a little while."

He led Ellen to the entrance of the old McDay house, which was almost hidden behind wisteria and acacia. After unlocking the front door, he guided her into the hall where a mahogany stair-case wound its way to the second floor. To their right a double set of sliding doors led into a cozy parlor filled with Tiffany glass lamps and Victorian furniture, oriental rugs, and porcelain urns.

The High Fiber Man closed the sliding doors behind them, and, motioning toward a brocade chair, he invited Ellen to sit down. She did so but with a sense of uneasiness in her movement. Her driver sat on a matching chair across the room and placed his briefcase on his lap. Suddenly his mouth was dry and his hands were shaking. He folded them on top of the briefcase and took a deep breath, which seemed to relax him. The light in the room was very dim. The street lamps cast lace shadows on the carpet between them.

"My name is Clarence McDay." The High Fiber Man's voice was very calm and soothing as though he were speaking to a sleepy child. "As a term of endearment, some people call me the High Fiber Man, but I'd prefer you to call me Clarence. It's much more business-like. And after all that's why you're here. Let me confess. My dear, I am not a chauffeur. I was not hired by your father, and I am not taking you to the Barbizon Hotel."

Ellen ran to the parlor doors and tried to force them, but they were locked. In her struggle she knocked over a chair.

"Shhh! Little Painted Lady must be very, very quiet." Clarence McDay pressed a finger against his small pink lips. "Too much noise will wake up Mother, and then she won't be able to go back to sleep again. I've got her on the second floor, now."

⊕

Ellen Smith was not exactly Clarence McDay's first kidnap victim. Two weeks before Ellen arrived in New York, Clarence had locked his mother on the second floor of their house. His intention was to stop her from giving away or shopping away what was left of the family fortune.

Mildred McDay had always been a generous spendthrift. "Spending money is my greatest plea-

74

sure." That's what she had always said before her son locked her up. "I can shop and shop and shop and never get tired of it. As long as I have a dollar to spend on myself or somebody deserving, I'm perfectly happy."

The rice cereal company had never been a breakfast cereal empire, but it had made Jonathan McDay a small fortune. The company, now a subsidiary of a larger cereal concern, was located in Babylon, New York, where Clarence was born and hoped never to return. His father sold the company one month and died of heart failure the next. Then Mildred McDay, who had always been bored in Babylon, moved to Manhattan with her fifteen-year-old son and four toy terriers which Clarence managed to poison one by one. He was allergic to fur.

Over the years Mildred McDay occupied her time by furnishing and refurnishing her four-story eighteen-room house on Barrow Street. She also gave lavish parties, commissioned works of art, and held Thursday afternoon teas.

"All this entertaining and subsidizing is terribly foolish," her son said. By the time I'm thirty there will be nothing left. I'll have to go to work."

"What a tragedy that will be," Mildred declared. "I suppose you think no one has ever worked before. How do you think your father made all this money?"

Early on Clarence showed signs of a strong financial sense. He entertained himself by dreaming up new ways to invest his father's money and curb his mother's spending. "For every dollar she spends, I will earn five." That was the rule he lived by until the strain of keeping up with Mildred's shopping sprees and generous donations was more than he could endure. Each week he received invoices for more paintings, more furniture, and more pieces of sculpture for the garden. Mildred worshipped the arts. And for those whose talents were, in her estimation, truly exceptional, she would often produce their plays, purchase their supplies, or sponsor their exhibitions.

Slowly Clarence watched the family fortune dwindle. He was always borrowing from his personal account to balance his mother's desires and generosities. "Just pay it, dear. I don't care how." Her sense of finance ended there.

At the age of thirty-four, Clarence, balding and still carrying his baby fat, decided to lock his mother up. On the evening before she was to make another sizable donation to the Museum of Modern Art, Clarence locked her on the second floor and refused to let her out. "Don't worry Mother," he said, speaking through the door, "I won't let you starve."

"You will never get away with this," she

screamed. "People will want to know where I am."

"Naturally, I will tell them you're dead." Clarence said, his tongue getting in the way of his words. That always happened when he got excited.

He attached three padlocks to the bedroom door and nailed boards over the outside shutters on the second floor. Then he announced his mother's death and cremation. "I intend to keep her rooms exactly as she left them," he told her friends. "I have sealed off that part of the house, and one day I will turn it into a museum." To create her last remains he mixed roasted cereal and cardboard ashes along with pumice stone and one of Mildred's favorite ceramic statues which he crushed in the back yard. Then on a sunny afternoon he invited all his mother's friends to scatter her ashes in Christopher Park.

"She was my inspiration for the society hostess in my epic novel, *Neither Here Nor There*," said Cherokee Rose as she flung a spoonful of ashes over the English ivy growing around the base of Sheridan's statue.

While Victor L. Russell played a taped recording of his sonata for cello that Mildred McDay had commissioned, Wickie Wormser, Cherokee's favorite writing student, made a brief statement. Wickie praised Mildred for generously financing her novel-in-progress. "She was overjoyed," Wickie added, "when I told her that she was the prototype for my main character, the good nun whose sister is a prostitute."

"She gave me this beautiful dress," said Maria la Hija de Jesús. "That's why I'm wearing it today. She convinced me I was a better actress than an actor. Now I get to wear pretty dresses all the time."

Two weeks after the service Maria la Hija de Jesús was leaving the Cherry Lane Theatre, where she was starring as a transexual junkie in a highly acclaimed play by a writer Mildred had subsidized. It was after midnight. A violent summer downpour had left the streets filled with leaves and dead limbs and the air charged with electricity. Maria looked up at the McDay house and crossed herself. Then she noticed that a shutter on the second floor had blown open and a pale face could faintly be seen at the window. "Jesús Cristo!" screamed Maria la Hija, running in the middle of the street. At the nearest telephone booth she called the High Fiber Man and told him she had seen a ghost.

"It was your mother!" Maria gasped. "Her face was in the window. I am not making this up."

"I see her all the time," Clarence said. "Even in the middle of the day. She stalks these hallways looking for a party or a bargain."

After hanging up the telephone, Clarence nailed the shutter closed with longer nails and stronger boards. While climbing down the ladder, he wondered how much longer his mother would live. At the age of sixty-four she had already suffered one heart attack as well as a light stroke. In spite of her fragile health, Clarence was afraid that she would live forever.

"There's only one thing to do," he told himself as he returned the ladder to the basement. "I must find someone who is capable of giving her a very innocent departure. So innocent that no one could possibly be suspected or blamed."

☙

"All I want you to do is entertain Mother," the High Fiber Man told Ellen. She was still trying to force the parlor doors but they were securely locked. "She's very, very ill and cannot leave the house, but she thinks she's perfectly healthy. All you need to do is keep her company."

Ellen felt her temperature rising uncontrollably. Her fingers began shaking as a cold sweat poured from her brow. Eye shadow, mascara, and rouge trickled down her face as Clarence led her to the top of the mahogany staircase and unlocked the door to his mother's rooms.

"Mother," he said, slowly opening the door. "I've found someone to live with you. She's a nice girl from the South. She'll take good care of you."

Mildred was already in bed reading. Her long grey hair hung over one eye in the style Veronica Lake had made fashionable. Her features were very delicate. Clearing a space on the bed, which was covered with books and magazines, she invited her visitor to sit. At first Ellen thought she was standing before Julie Harris. She rushed into the room. Clarence closed the door behind her and locked it with three locks.

"You must not allow my son to frighten you," Mildred said. "He's not well. I don't think he's ever been well."

Pointing to a calendar with the dates X'ed off in green ink, she told Ellen that she'd been locked up for sixteen days. "He's told everyone that I'm dead," she explained while slipping out of bed and into a silk wrapper. "He took great pleasure in showing me my obituary in the *Times*. And meanwhile, here I am, starving to death. Three times a day he feeds me old, stale cereal because we still receive a discount on it and very ripe bananas because they're the least expensive fruit available. Clarence, you see, is afraid of running out of money. That's why he turned the air conditioning off. When he finds a penny on the street it makes his day. He has piggy banks filled with coins he's found on the streets, and piggy banks filled with coins he's found in the park. He's terrified that he'll have to go to work one day. That's been his lifelong fear. One of them, anyway."

Without warning Clarence opened the door and shoved Ellen's suitcase into the room as though it were food for hungry lions. "Oh!" Mildred calmly swept the lock of hair from her eye. "My son seems to have found your suitcase. How thoughtful of him." Then she searched for a pair of clean sheets while Ellen sat down and cried.

Mildred made a bed on a small couch and attempted to console her unexpected guest. "One day Clarence will tire of this little game of his and let us out. Until then we must stay alive and well."

Ellen cried herself to sleep.

The next morning the door opened slightly and a breakfast tray with two bowls of cereal and two bananas came sliding into the room. "I would kill for an electric fan and a cup of coffee," Mildred said, as she set the table.

After breakfast Ellen spent an hour applying her make-up and watching it melt on her face. "I apologize for the oppressive heat and the lack of fresh air," Mildred said. "My son has nailed every window shut. Therefore, we must stay as calm as possible to keep from passing out."

Then she doused Ellen with expensive perfume

and gave her a tour of the second floor. There were three very large rooms. The one they shared was furnished in Chinese Chippendale and potted palms. The walls were covered with modern paintings and photographs of Mildred and her friends. The other rooms were filled with paintings that had never been hung and pieces of sculpture that had never been shown. "I'm afraid I have done nothing but spend money on myself and talented friends," Mildred confessed. "Not that that isn't good enough, mind you, but surely I could have thought of something else to go along with it. Maybe I should have been an actress, for example."

"I intend to be the next Julie Harris," said Ellen.

"That's a very impressive ambition," Mildred replied. "But are you talented? So many people who end up in New York are not, you know. Talent is a very rare thing nowadays."

That afternoon Mildred listened attentively, sometimes with her eyes closed, as Ellen read *The Glass Menagerie*. She changed her voice with each character, and at times she leaped to her feet to perform a piece of action.

"You're phrasing is quite good," Mildred told her. "Perhaps it's even beyond your understanding. But I think you need to concentrate more on the classics or you'll never lose that accent, and my dear, dear Ellen it simply must go and go fast unless you intend to build a career on Mr. Tennessee Williams." She searched her bookcase for a copy of *Romeo and Juliet*.

Toward evening, after Ellen had read all of Juliet's soliloquies, Clarence's footsteps were heard on the stairs. He rapped on the door. "Little Painted Lady," he called. "Time for tea." He opened the door only wide enough for Ellen to squeeze through. "We must call Daddy," he said, escorting her into the parlor. "Just tell him his little girl is all right. It would be very unwise to say anything else."

Dressed in his secondhand tuxedo and Red Ball tennis shoes, he sat on a chaperon couch and sipped tea while listening to Ellen talk to her father. Her voice trembled as she spoke to him. After hanging up, she broke into tears. Mascara ran down her crimson cheeks. Her blue eyelids fluttered.

"Little Painted Lady." Clarence addressed his victim in a soft voice. "You will be allowed to call home every evening at this time." He smiled. There were spaces between his front teeth. His hand checked to make sure that his briefcase was still sitting upright between his feet. "Only when you do what I want you to do will you be allowed to leave."

"Believe me I'll do anything you want," said

Ellen. "I'll even sleep with you every night if that's what it takes."

"I sleep alone!" Clarence spoke in a stern voice as though defending his honor. He reached for the briefcase. "I have always slept alone, and I will go on sleeping alone. I'm used to it now."

"Then what do you want?" asked Ellen.

"I want you to K-I-L-L M-O-T-H-E-R." Clarence giggled with his mouth closed. He held the briefcase upright on his legs and squeezed the handle with both hands. For a few moments he seemed to choke on his own breath.

It took Ellen several seconds to realize what Clarence had spelled. "Kill her? Why?" She was almost unable to speak. "I've never killed anything."

"That's why I chose you." Clarence opened his briefcase and peeped into it as he spoke. "You'll be able to think of a way that's completely innocent, just like you. And you will be able to do it without really doing it yourself. Perhaps you could help her have an accident while you're keeping her company. That way no one can be blamed."

"Why don't *you* do it?" Ellen was suddenly very cold.

"Don't be silly, Little Painted Lady!" Clarence hugged his briefcase. "After all. She *is* my mother."

84

Every evening at six o'clock Clarence rapped on the door and Ellen was invited into the parlor. Every evening she called her father with a favorable report of life in New York. Every evening her voice trembled. She cried after hanging up the phone, and her make-up ran with the tears. After five days she stopped painting her face. She stopped combing her hair and reading aloud to Mildred. But she did not stop crying. She begged Clarence to have a heart.

"That's my problem, dear," he finally confessed while staring at his folded hands. "I do have a heart. I wouldn't have allowed Mother to enjoy so much money for so long a time had I not had a heart. The problem is I have always had too much heart."

"And now you have none at all," Ellen said.

"And now I have less than before." Clarence corrected her. "Time to go back upstairs, dear. Please remember what you're here for."

"You must keep yourself up," Mildred McDay advised Ellen. "When we get out of here we'll want to look our best. That's why I brush my hair one thousand times in the morning and one thousand times at night. That's why I continue to wear a bit of make-up and get dressed each day. And so should you."

But Ellen was unable to follow Mildred's example. She spent her mornings watching television and entertaining thoughts of hopelessness. She spent her afternoons playing solitaire and dreading her six o'clock appointment in the parlor.

"What does he ask of you?" Mildred inquired during the second week of Ellen's captivity. She did not answer. She was tired. Her eyes seem to be slowly disappearing inside her head, and she had almost stopped talking altogether.

"I said, what does he ask of you?"

Ellen fixed her glassy and vacant eyes on Mildred. "I'd like to comb your hair," Ellen said. "It's so pretty."

As she combed Mildred's hair, she jerked her head from side to side. "What are you trying to do?" asked Mildred. "Break my neck?"

Ellen did not answer. She dropped the comb on the floor and left it there.

The next morning when the breakfast tray was shoved inside the room, Ellen pulled a large button off her winter coat and hid it in the cereal.

"What's this?" asked Mildred, spooning the button from her cereal bowl. "Is someone trying to choke me?"

"Yes," answered Ellen.

"Who?" asked Mildred.

"I am." Ellen broke into tears. "But I don't know how."

"So that's it," Mildred whispered. "He's brought

86

you here to kill me. He can't do it himself, of course."

"He wants it to be innocent," Ellen sobbed. "He wants me to do it *accidently on purpose,* so if we're found out, no one will be blamed.

"Well, that makes a whole lot of sense now, doesn't it?" Mildred flashed an ironic smile. "Only Clarence would think of something like that."

"I can't do it," Ellen said.

"Oh yes you can," Mildred assured her. "And I will help you. I've had my life. I don't need to live any longer, but you're just beginning. Suppose I tell you something about myself." She tossed her Veronica Lake hair out of her eye before going on. "I shock easily. I frighten easily. I have often lost my breath when suddenly surprised by someone on the street. That's just my nature, and my son is well aware of it. Now listen to me carefully. If you should bring to me a portion, not all, of the contents of my son's brief-case, and if I should gaze upon what I know it contains but have never allowed myself to really see, I'm sure I would die of shock. There are many things I know about my son. Many things that I have never told anyone."

After that when Ellen was summoned to the parlor to call home, she could not take her eyes off the briefcase, even when she was telling her father that she was well and happy. Every evening she looked for the slightest opportunity to carry out Mildred's plan. She noticed that Clarence seemed to trust her a little more each day. He sometimes briefly turned his back on her while pouring tea. Once he even crossed the room without keeping his eyes fastened to hers.

"I don't expect to be here much longer," she announced after one of her phone calls. "But I have lost so much weight, and I don't want anyone to see me this thin. Do you think I could have some vanilla wafers."

"Graham crackers, dear." Clarence smiled and went into the kitchen.

Ellen rushed to the briefcase and opened it. For a moment her heart almost stopped. For a moment, which seems like hours, she was unable to breathe deeply. The briefcase contained a white cloth folded neatly with two large safety pins attached to it. Under the cloth was an assortment of photographs, the likes of which Ellen had never seen. In some of them Clarence was completely naked, in others he was wearing a white diaper over which his baby fat hung in suspension. Women dressed in leather were handcuffing him. Muscle men with hard, oiled bodies were turning him over their knees.

Ellen grabbed a handful of pictures and stuffed them into her bodice. When Clarence returned to the room, she was lying on the floor. Her head was swimming. Her lips were quivering. "I almost fainted," she told him as he helped her to a chair. His hands felt soft and damp on her arms.

"You need a bit of sugar, dear. I haven't been giving you enough, have I." Clarence placed a graham cracker into her hands. She didn't want to touch anything his hands had touched. The thought of putting the graham cracker in her mouth made her stomach weak. He forced her to eat it. As she slowly began to chew, her mouth filled with liquid. The graham cracker tasted as though it had been soaked in vinegar. She swallowed it, but it came back up again.

"Mustn't ruin such a pretty dress, Miss," Clarence said. He left the room to get a wet towel. When he returned, Ellen was standing up.

"I must lie down now," she told him. "I'll be all right in the morning."

The next morning she washed and rolled her hair while Mildred slept. She carefully packed her suitcase and counted her traveler's checks. She spent the morning watching television, and in the afternoon she agreed to read Shakespeare's sonnets to Mildred.

"That was very beautiful," Mildred said, after Ellen closed the book. "Your voice is stronger. There's more color in it today too. Why is that, I wonder?"

Ellen answered by placing an envelope on

89

Mildred's lap. "Please don't open this while I'm in the room. That's all I ask."

That evening in the parlor Clarence listened to Ellen chatting with her father. Her mood was light, yet there was a strange tension in her voice that caused Clarence to laugh nervously at everything she said. After the phone call he poured tea, and while they drank in silence they listened to Mildred's footsteps. She crossed the floor first to turn the television off and then to turn it back on again. Then to turn the radio on and then to turn it off. Back and forth she traveled across the second floor. Ellen followed each step. She stared at the ceiling. The High Fiber Man stared at the ceiling also.

"Is something about to happen, dear?"

Ellen shrugged her shoulders and sipped her tea. She tried not to look up.

Soon Mildred's steps changed directions. She walked toward the front windows, and for a few minutes there was no sound of movement.

"I think it's time for you to go back upstairs." The High Fiber Man stood, ready to escort her.

"Not just yet, please," begged Ellen. The urgency in her voice persuaded Clarence to allow her to stay. Together they listened as Mildred began pacing again. Soon she started toward the bathroom. Her steps were deliberate, more determined in their direction. She opened the door.

In the parlor Ellen could hear the hinges squeak. For a moment there was silence again. Then came a faint gasp followed by the sound of Mildred's body hitting the floor.

"It's done!" Ellen shouted, springing to her feet. "It's over. I can leave now."

"Not just yet, my dear," Clarence silently clapped his hands. "We must make sure, mustn't we."

For half an hour they sat listening for more footsteps. They stared at the floor. Occasionally their eyes meet on their way to the ceiling or back down again. An hour passed. No sound was heard from the second floor.

"Please, may I go now," Ellen begged. "It's after eight o'clock."

"First, we must make a small inspection." Clarence smiled and stood up. He escorted Ellen to the second floor. He unlocked the door and opened it. "Mother," he called cheerfully. "Mother! Are you there?" He walked into the dark room. A thin trail of light coming from the bathroom sliced the darkness like a sharp blade.

"Mother, are you in the bathroom?" Clarence walked cautiously toward the half-opened door. Ellen followed him.

Suddenly, he stopped. "Why, Mother," he said sympathetically. "You *are* there. You've fallen

91

down, haven't you. I wonder what made you do that."

Mildred was lying on the floor. Her face was partially visible under her hair. Scattered over the bath mat and in the sink were the photographs of Clarence. When he saw them, he attempted to hide his laughter with feigned sadness. "Oh, poor, poor Mommie. She found out about her little boy, didn't she?"

"This was her idea," Ellen said, inching her way toward the door. "She asked me to find out what was in your briefcase."

Clarence removed the photographs and put them in his pocket. "The truth is so very painful sometimes," he told Ellen as he closed the bathroom door behind him. The bedroom was dark. Ellen could not see him, but she could feel his breath on her face, and then his fleshy lips brush across her cheek. She backed up slowly until her heels touched her suitcase.

"I always wanted to tell her about her little boy," Clarence confessed. "But I was afraid it would kill her. She should have never asked you to meddle in my private things. That was *her* mistake, wasn't it?"

"It was her mistake and she paid for it." Ellen almost didn't recognize her own voice. "It's time for me to go now," she reminded him. She picked up her suitcase.

"First we must celebrate." With his hands on her shoulders, the High Fiber Man led Ellen Smith out of the dark room and down the stairs. He was now ready to carry out the last of his carefully laid plans.

In the parlor he opened a special wine. He poured himself a glass from the bottle and emptied the rest of it into a crystal decanter containing a small amount of yellow powder. "I even washed the limousine this week," he told Ellen as he poured her drink from the decanter. "Somehow I just knew."

While sipping his wine, Clarence McDay noticed Ellen's beige dress. "Oh, wear your polka dots, dear," he said. "And paint your face the way you used to. Put on your pretty straw hat, too. It doesn't matter that it's dark outside. Come on, dress up pretty for dear, ole Clarence."

He sat down and watched Ellen apply her makeup; first a pale pink foundation, then cherry-red rouge and lipstick, followed by three shades of glittering eyeshadow. After carefully setting her face with powder, she opened her suitcase and undressed before her captor. He licked his lips and laughed while she put on her polka dot dress and then her hat. "Little Painted Lady," he said pouring another glass of wine from the decanter. "This is the way I will always remember you." Ellen drank the second glass of wine hurriedly.

She was beginning to think she would never be allowed to leave.

The High Fiber Man took Ellen's empty glass and studied it for a moment. "I guess we can be going now," he said. Offering his arm, he escorted her through the parlor and out the front door. Once outside Ellen was overcome by the fresh air. Her lungs ached. She was lightheaded. The lamp posts swayed before her. On the bottom step she tripped, almost collapsed.

"It must be the wine, dear," Clarence said, supporting her to the curb. "I forget you're not accustomed to drinking."

He helped her into the limousine, making sure that she sat on the right-hand side, with her knees against the door and the suitcase on the seat next to her. Then he drove to the corner and turned toward midtown. By the time they reached Fourteenth Street, Ellen was sleeping. "Little Painted Lady is so very tired," Clarence said. He drove directly to the Port Authority Bus Terminal and stopped on the curb. Then he woke her up. "Where did you say you were going, Miss?"

Ellen, startled, tried to sit up. The terminal lights were blinding. She was very sleepy, and could hardly speak.

"I'm going to the Barbizon Hotel," she said.

"First, I've been hired to give you a little tour," her driver announced. "Your father's idea." He took her for a spin through Times Square and the theatre district.

Ellen struggled to keep her eyes open as the High Fiber Man read the marquees aloud. "You're going to be the next Julie Harris," he said as they stopped briefly in front of the Shubert Theatre.

"Yes I am," Ellen managed to say. "That's my dream."

"When you're famous I'll tell everyone I was the first to show you the town." The High Fiber Man then sped off toward Fifth Avenue. He pointed out St. Patrick's Cathedral, Rockefeller Center, and Saks Fifth Avenue. On they sped, past the Public Library, Lord and Taylor's, and the Empire State Building. Finally, they came to the Washington Arch, still marred with graffiti.

"It's just beautiful, isn't it?" he said.

"Yes, it is," Ellen replied, trying hard to stay awake. "I've only seen it in pictures."

Then the High Fiber Man headed back uptown on the East side. Ellen Smith slept the entire way. At the Barbizon Hotel he parked in front of the canopy and leaned over the front seat. "Better wake up Miss." He gently tugged on Ellen's arms. "You've been having a very bad dream. The things you told me in your sleep shouldn't be repeated, you know."

Ellen sat up in jerks. "What did I say? Where am I?"

"You're at the Barbizon Hotel," the High Fiber Man told her. "You have slept for a very long time."

He opened the door and helped her out of the limousine. Then he turned her over to the doorman. "See that she gets the best," he said. "This young lady is going to be very famous one day."

✿

Back on Barrow Street, Mildred McDay was wondering if it was safe to leave the house. She had no idea what time it was, but for what she judged to be forty-five minutes she had heard no sounds in the house. Slowly she crept across the second floor bedroom and down the stairs, occasionally stopping to listen.

Across the street Maria la Hija de Jesús was leaving the Cherry Lane Theatre. For a moment she stopped to cross herself in front of the McDay house. Just as she made the sign of the cross, the front door opened and Mildred came tearing down the steps. "Help me!" she screamed. "Help me! He thinks I'm dead, but I'm not. I was just pretending. Now, get me to the precinct, fast."

She rushed up to Maria la Hija who was sitting in the middle of the street. Her mouth was hanging wide open, and her eyes were fixed on Mildred's face and long grey hair. "Can you hear me?" Mildred said, lightly slapping Maria on both cheeks. "Try to understand. I am not dead. I have been alive all this time, and something wonderful has happened."

For a long time Maria la Hija de Jesús was unable to move. Finally she managed to close her mouth and then, still in a state of shock, she whispered. "What has happened that's so wonderful?" And Mildred replied:

"I have discovered the next Julie Harris."

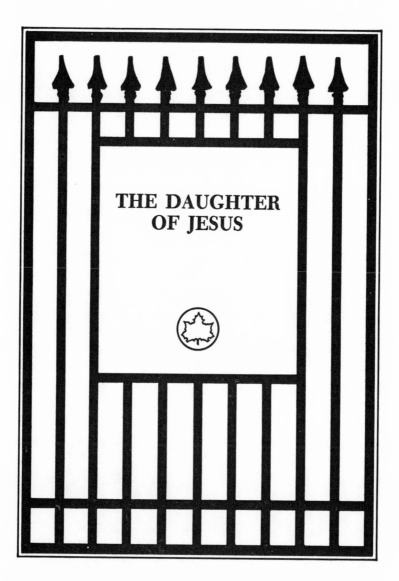

THE DAUGHTER
OF JESUS

Maria la Hija de Jesús, one of off-off Broadway's most celebrated stars, often worked
as a volunteer at the Riverview Nursing Home,
where she read stories to the aged and occasionally took the more agile residents on walking tours
through the Village. The walking tours always
included stops at the Village Laundry, where Maria's photo was hanging on the wall, the Yellow
Parrot Cafe, where Maria's photo was hanging on
the wall, and every theatre and cabaret where
Maria had performed or would perform and where
her eight-by-ten was or soon would be hanging
on the wall.

Recently she had been asked to host an evening
of entertainment for the residents of Riverview,
and after days of thought she decided to take
them on a fantasy trip to Spain. The evening was
approved by the director of the home, Mr. Stanley
Zemsky, whose ideas regarding the care of the
aged were being questioned by the board.

"Our senior citizens have active imaginations,"

101

Mr. Zemsky informed his board of directors. "Maria la Hija de Jesús, one of our most creative volunteers, has seen to that."

On the evening of the fantasy trip a hint of autumn arrived but did not cool Maria's raw nerves. Never had she been so nervous, not even on the opening of her first off-off Broadway play. "This is an experiment," she confessed to Joanie Maples, the new night nurse who was helping convert a long corridor into the interior of a passenger plane. Folding chairs with seatbelts attached had been lined up in pairs with an aisle down the middle. Aerial photographs had been hung on the walls, and a movie projector had been set up at the back of the make-believe aircraft. At the last minute Maria and Nurse Maples, both of whom were dressed as flight attendants, struggled to unfold a movie screen on which two in-flight travel films would be shown.

"Isn't this an odd way to entertain old people?" asked the cheerful young nurse. She had just graduated from nursing school, and this was her first job.

"I said this was an experiment, didn't I?" Maria had always hated questions.

"Have you ever been to Spain?" Nurse Maples wanted to know.

"Not exactly," Maria answered sharply.

"Well, have you or haven't you?"

"Yes I have, and no I haven't." Maria was almost shouting. "What else can I say?"

"Well, where are you from anyway, New York?"

"Yes and no," Maria answered in a tired voice. "I have had two births. First I was born in Mexico City, and later on I was born again right here in Manhattan."

"Born again?" Nurse Maple frowned as she steadied the screen. "Are you talking about religion?"

"No I'm not!" Maria said. "Now don't get me vexed. I'm talking about fantasy. Isn't that why we're here, anyway?"

Guillermo Garcia was born in Mexico City, but Maria la Hija de Jesús was born in an all-night beauty salon in Manhattan's East Village. Guillermo, sometimes called Mo, was giving a foil frost at three a.m. when an irate customer appeared at the receptionist's desk.

"I can't comb it," the inebriated lady screamed, pointing to Doughnut, an overweight, punked-out stylist who had *ruined* her. "It's all his fault."

"Sometimes hair needs time to settle after a heavy styling," the oriental receptionist explained.

"I'm not leaving," the customer shouted, "until someone puts me back together again. But I don't want *him* to do it." She pointed to Doughnut again. "And I don't want her. And I don't want him, or her, or that person way over there."

"Who do you want, then?" the receptionist asked.

"I don't know," said the woman, swaying on her feet. "Can't you see that I'm upset beyond the ability to make a rational decision? All I know was I don't want a man to touch me, and I don't want a woman to touch me, and I don't want a child to touch me either."

"How about a combination?" the receptionist suggested.

"Fine," said the intoxicated customer as she sat down to wait.

The receptionist left the desk, and a few minutes later she returned wearing Mo's shirt, pants, and tie. Shortly, Mo, wearing the receptionist's skirt and blouse, skipped into the waiting room with a scarf tied around his head. "Maria la Hija de Jesús, a sus ordenes, Señora. I have been asked to restore your beauty and good humor. This should not be too difficult, yes?"

"Am I supposed to look like this?" the customer screamed, pulling on the ends of her hair.

"No one should look like you," Maria squealed. "But I will fix." She twirled and flounced her skirt and skipped back to her station.

"At last I've found someone who knows something about hair," the customer said on her way out. "Now, I know who to ask for next time."

That day, the twenty-fifth of July, marked the conception and birth of Maria la Hija de Jesús. Soon she was the most popular all-night stylist in the salon. Everyone wanted an appointment with "that nice Spanish girl, Maria-Something-or-Other."

⊕

"Don't tell these old people I was born in Mexico City," Maria la Hija told the nurse assisting her with the make-believe trip. "Let them think Spain. They'll enjoy the trip more if they think I know the country. And believe me, I know how to play along. I'm not an actress for nothing."

"Why did you decide to become an actress?" Nurse Maples asked. The innocence in her voice irritated Maria's already sensitive nerves.

"It was an accident, totally unexplainable," Maria said, working to maintain her patience. "Most people have better sense than to ask me that."

"Why?" the nurse whined. "I don't understand."

"For obvious reasons too hard to explain," Maria informed her. "Now don't ask me anything else tonight?"

"Did you always want to be an actress?"

"Are you listening to me or what?" Maria raised

her voice. "Don't get me angry before a performance. You'll be very sorry if you do."

As the aged residents arrived in the lobby of
Riverview, Mr. Zemsky, dressed in a pilot's uniform, passed out counterfeit airplane tickets and
boarding passes. The passengers were boarded
one by one and ushered to their assigned seats.

Then Maria stood before the seated passengers,
thirty-two in all, and delivered her first speech:

"Toreador Tours welcomes you to Flight Number 103 to Madrid. Our flight time will be ap-
proximately forty-five minutes. Please make sure
that your seat belts are securely fastened as our
pilot has already advised us of strong turbulence
on this transatlantic crossing."

Nurse Maples passed out air sickness bags while
Maria pointed to the emergency exits. Then she
held an air sickness bag over her mouth and
walked up and down the aisle while staring into
the faces of the passengers. "Please press these
waterproof receptacles to your mouths and hold
them there until you are relieved of sickness."
She spoke without removing the bag from her
mouth. "Then neatly fold the top of the necessary
receptacle and place it in the hand of a friendly
flight attendant. I'm sure you will be able to
recognize one."

"What if you don't feel sick, do you have to
use them?" asked Victor L. Russell. Maria la Hija

106

sometimes called him "the world's oldest living composer."

"What a sensible question, Mr. Russell." Maria removed the bag from her mouth. "Who knows the answer?"

Mrs. Alice Grisbee, whose sagging eyelids obscured her vision, raised her hand and spoke out. "If you're not sick you don't have to use your bags. That's what I've been told."

"What we have here is a sensible answer to a sensible question," exclaimed Maria. Her arms akimbo, she paraded up and down the aisle like a beauty contestant. "Did everyone hear what Mrs. Grisbee just said?"

"I left my teeth in my room," whined Mr. Elmer Butler, who got his start in silent movies and was later forced out of the business due to the tone of his voice.

"Too bad about your teeth, Mr. Butler," Maria said as she unraveled an oxygen tube. "You'll just have to do without them until we return."

"Are we going to eat on this flight?" asked Mrs. Oscar Wallace, a stout octogenarian who had lived in the home for five years.

"Dinner will be served shortly after take off," Nurse Maples announced.

"Food Service has answered this very important question," replied Maria la Hija de Jesús. "Thank you so much, Food Service. Now we may proceed with our oxygen masks located just under our seats. Please familiarize yourself with your breathing apparatus at once." Suddenly Maria stomped her feet. "Mr. Weinberger!" she shouted. "I can see your mind drifting off. Please remain alert at all times."

Holding the oxygen mask and tubing above her head, she waited until she had the attention of all the passengers, and then she proceeded with her next set of instructions:

"Now, carefully, place your breathing device over your nose and secure it with the elasticized head band." She paused. "That's correct. Very good, passengers, very, very good. Please practice this procedure until you are comfortable with it. You never know when cabin pressure will be lost and additional oxygen will be needed."

"I don't like putting anything over my nose," complained Mr. Petigo. He suffered from a deviated septum.

"Then place the mask over your mouth and breathe deeply Mr. Petigo." Maria demonstrated this procedure. "Preliminary attention to these security devices could save your life in the case of a sudden emergency."

Some of the passengers, with oxygen masks in place, turned around to look at each other and laugh. "I can't recognize anybody under these things," said Miss Jane Westly, a retired librarian. "Where's my sweet roommate?"

"Here I am, Lessie-Wessie," shouted Mr. Butler. He stood up and the chair he was fastened to came with him.

"You are not Miss Westly's roommate, Mr. Butler." Maria spoke sympathetically. "You would like to be, I'm sure, but unfortunately, cohabitation is not allowed at Riverview."

"Is that so," answered Mr. Butler. He had escaped his chair and was walking up the aisle. "I believe there's a lot that goes on around here that nobody knows about."

"Quiet, Elmer!" whispered Miss Westly. "You don't have to tell everything you know."

Nurse Maples returned Mr. Butler to his proper place on the aircraft and securely fastened his seat belt.

Mr. Zemsky looked at his watch.

"What does cohabitation mean?" the nurse asked.

"Prepare for take-off," announced Maria la Hija as if answering the nurse's question. "Please remember that no one is allowed in the aisles until our pilot has turned off the Fasten Your Seat Belts Sign. Now passengers, please extinguish your smoking materials at once."

"Smoking isn't allowed at Riverview," shouted Mr. Petigo.

"Mr. Petigo!" Maria pointed her finger at the aged resident. "How many times must I tell you that we are no longer at Riverview Nursing Home. We're on an airplane bound for Madrid. Please try to remember this, as it will make the trip much more exciting."

For a moment the passengers were silent. Maria took a seat next to Mrs. Sally Pace, who was sitting in a wheelchair. "Mrs. Pace, I pray that your wheels are locked," Maria said as she fastened her own seat belt. "If they aren't, there's nothing I can do about it now."

"I live with my wheels locked," Mrs. Pace confessed.

"So should everyone," Maria replied.

The overhead lights flashed on and off as an engine was heard roaring in the distance. In the back of the airplane Nurse Maples was starting the movie projector. Shortly an aerial view of Manhattan appeared on the screen. The picture was very shaky.

"Now we're in the air," Maria announced. "Look there's the Empire State Building. My God! We almost hit it."

"Don't let us crash," screamed Mrs. Alice Grisbee. With index fingers she lifted her sagging eyelids in order to see the screen. "Can't we turn around? I'm ready to go home now."

"Too late for home, Mrs. Grisbee," said Maria

la Hija. "We're already flying over Long Island. Watch the screen and you'll know exactly where we are."

"The picture's jumping too bad," shouted Mr. Ernie Watson, a retired school teacher. "It makes me dizzy to look at it."

"Then you better locate your air-sickness bag immediately," Maria warned him. "You're probably going to be the first to need it. Please try not to make a mess."

Soon the picture was calmer. Land was replaced by a seascape dotted with islands. Nurse Maples turned on the lights in the back of the corridor and prepared the beverage trays. Maria stood before the passengers. An Atlantic seascape was projected onto her uniform. "Today our complimentary beverage is sangria." As she spoke a dolphin leaped from her uniform and onto the screen. "Please sip slowly and remain seated at all times," she advised the passengers while serving the drinks. "Turbulence can be expected as we are crossing the Atlantic at a very low altitude in order to observe life on the surface of the water. Watch for the turtles! They'll be swimming along very soon."

"Have you ever been to Madrid?" Victor L. Russell asked, when Maria served him sangria in a paper cup.

"Not exactly, Mr. Russell," Maria confessed,

"but don't worry I have been on many flights to Spain." ⊕

Guillermo Garcia's entire family was born in Mexico City. His mother, Estrella, was ashamed of her mestizo heritage and compensated by telling everyone that she was born into an upper-class family in Madrid.

Estrella, a diminutive ton of energy, took pride in her appearance, particularly her fair complexion, which she attributed to aristocratic blood. To guard against tanning she wore hats, scarves, colored stockings, and cotton gloves into the Mexican sun. Bareback dresses and bathing suits were not included in her wardrobe.

Because of Estrella's persistence, Guillermo quickly became a child star on Mexican television. Estrella saved her son's salary until he was twelve years old. Then she left her Mexican husband and escaped to the United States where she was sure her son would instantly become a movie star. They had been in Los Angeles only a few weeks when Estrella realized that she was running out of money.

"There was only one thing to do," she told her son. "I will find us a new father."

She dyed her hair blond and went out every night until she met Sidney Lang, a businessman of means. "I am the blond bombshell you have always wanted," Estrella told her future husband. "My skin is white because I am not Mexican or Puerto Rican or anything that lives in those *horrible* South American countries. I am from Madrid. I grew up in a small castle. My brother is a marquis. And I am the only one who can make you happy."

Mo's complexion, slightly darker than his mother's, had always been one of Estrella's concerns. After she became engaged to Sidney Lang, she no longer allowed her son to lie in the sun or wear shorts. She no longer allowed him to swim, even on the shady side of the pool, or go to the beach except for a few minutes just after sunset. To lighten his complexion she experimented on him with skin bleaches and creams as well as pancake foundations and face powders. She also tweezed his eyebrows to keep them from growing together over his nose.

After marrying Sidney Lang, Estrella and her son would "visit relatives in Madrid" at least once a year. "My family is very prejudiced," she told Sidney. "They would disown me if they knew I was married to an American. I cannot tell them yet."

She would schedule her flights during the day when Sidney was in the office or during the early morning when he was sleeping. At the last minute she would call a taxi.

"What airline?" the driver would ask.

"Mexicana," Estrella would whisper as if her husband were listening.

☺

On the dinner flight to Madrid, Maria la Hija and Nurse Maples began serving paella on TV trays. "What airline is this?" Miss Faye Longmere, a small woman with make-up pressed into her wrinkles, wanted to know.

"We're flying Mexicana tonight," Maria said as she positioned a tray in front of Mr. Petigo, who was slightly hard of hearing.

"I thought we were going to Madrid," he shouted.

"We are," answered Maria. "Mexicana has sometimes been known to fly there."

☺

Sidney Lang discovered his wife's true heritage by following her to the airport and buying a ticket on the same plane. While in flight he moved from first class to coach where Estrella and Guillermo were sitting.

"Why are you going to Mexico City?" he asked.

"Why are you following me?" Estrella answered.

"Have you ever been to Spain?" he asked.

"Yes and no," she answered.

"Well have you or haven't you?" he demanded.

"Don't ask me another question," Estrella

screamed. "You'll get me upset before we land, and then you will be very sorry."

Estrella received a small divorce settlement, and with the money she enrolled in beauty school. "We must have some means of support until you, my son, are a star again," she told Guillermo. Then she decided to enroll him in the same program. They were the first mother/son team to graduate from La Escuela Belleza de Los Angeles.

Because of his heavy accent, no casting director would consider Guillermo for a part. At the age of eighteen he moved to New York where he was sure his career would be rejuvenated. Over and over he was cast as Chief Sitting Bull in *Annie Get Your Gun*. On the dinner-theatre circuit he became identified with the role, and by the time he was thirty he had performed it in twenty different productions across the country.

He was getting nowhere fast and was ready to give up acting altogether, when, unannounced and totally unexpected, Maria la Hija de Jesús entered his life. In the first month of her existence she was photographed for the cover of *Outer Limits Magazine*. That covershot led to a part in an off-off Broadway play called *Woman on the Make*, which in turn led to several appearances in films by a director of softcore pornography. Before long Mildred McDay, patroness of the arts, insisted that Maria audition for the role of the

lesbian countess in a musical version of *Dracula.*
That role brought Maria la Hija de Jesús overnight
success.

"My son, the daughter of Jesus. He is a very
famous actress," Estrella bragged to all her beauty
salon regulars. "She was born in Madrid."

☻

"Madrid is a very large city," Maria explained
as she removed dinner trays. "We will be landing
there shortly."

"What a pretty girl you are," Mr. Tyson, a
retired clergyman, said when Maria bent over to
collect his tray. He cupped his hands on her nylon
breasts and squeezed.

"Mr. Tyson," shrieked Maria la Hija. "You're
a dirty old man, no?"

"Si, si, señorita," Mr. Tyson confessed. "Meet
me somewhere."

"Turbulence!" Maria shouted, practically shaking Mr. Tyson out of his chair. "Our pilot has
issued a warning." She ran to the back of the
plane and shook the projector. Spouting whales
were thrown onto the walls, ceiling, and floor.

"Turbulence!" Mr. Zemsky announced from the
back of the aircraft.

Maria ran down the aisle shaking the seats from
behind. "We have encountered high pressure
winds while flying at a low altitude," she shouted.

116

"Passengers, prepare your air sickness bags for immediate use."

Nurse Maple turned on an industrial floor fan. A strong wind whipped through the corridor, shaking the movie screen and blowing napkins off the dinner trays.

"There goes my kleenex," screamed Miss Longmere as she got up to retrieve it. Maria forced her back into her seat.

Mr. Petigo pretended to lose his dinner. "I've evacuated into my air sickness bag," he said, holding up the evidence. "Now what do I do?"

"We are experiencing a loss of cabin pressure," Mr. Zemsky shouted. "Please remain in your seats and prepare to use your oxygen masks at once."

"Get me out of here!" screamed Mrs. Sally Pace from her wheelchair on the front row. "It's too windy. I just had my hair done."

"Be patient," shouted Maria la Hija. "We're almost there."

A few moments later the turbulence subsided and the aircraft landed safely in Madrid. The passengers, wearing oxygen masks and carrying air sickness bags, exited the airplane for a flamenco demonstration in the lobby. The dancers were wearing traditional costumes.

As Maria la Hija de Jesús watched her friends demonstrate the fine points of flamenco, Guillermo realized why he identified with the female

117

dancers rather than the male. He felt closer to their sense of drama and to the movement of their hips and upper bodies. He also liked their dresses.

"Let's face it," Maria said to Nurse Maples. "I'd wear anything that had a ruffle on it."

"That's just the way some people are, I guess," replied the unsuspecting nurse.

For a few seconds Mo sank into a deep reverie. He had recently been contemplating the necessity for a sex change. His medical doctor had advised him to proceed with the preliminary treatments, the silicone injections, the hormones, and the electrolysis. But for some reason Mo could not yet explain, he would not allow himself to follow his doctor's advice.

Released from his reverie, he studied the Spanish dancers again. This time he identified more with the men. Their hips were slim and their backs were severely arched as they stood with their feet placed close together and their arms curved before them. Guillermo stood up and imitated the pose. It felt comfortable.

"I think I know someone who would like to take flamenco lessons," Maria la Hija said.

"Who?" the nurse asked. "You're not talking about me are you?"

"I wouldn't dare talk about you," Maria replied. "I don't even know why I talk *to* you."

"You haven't told me why you decided to become an actress," the nurse complained. "I'm *still* waiting."

"Listen to me, once and for all." Maria forced sweetness into her voice. "I don't know why I do what I do except that other people seem to like it. If I knew more than that I'd have told you long ago, believe me I would have."

The nurse was silenced.

Maria quickly turned her attention back to the dancers.

Mr. Tyson was dancing with Carmen Sanchez, and Jose Montejo was dancing with Miss Faye Longmere, who was lifting her skirt flirtatiously above her knees. Castanets and red roses had been distributed, and the aged residents were clicking out rhythms of their own while stomping around the lobby with the Spanish dancers.

"You have to wear very good shoes to dance the flamenco," Miss Westly observed. "The bottoms of my feet are burning."

"That means you are very passionate, Señora," shouted Juan Marquez.

"Why, I don't dare tell Mr. Butler you said that." Miss Westly giggled as Juan twirled her around the room. "He's already so jealous he can't stand it."

Sitting on the edge of the receptionist's desk, Maria la Hija and Nurse Maples watched Mr.

119

Zemsky and the residents of Riverview as they tackled the flamenco. "We're not going to need that second travel film after all," Maria decided. "Nor will we need the return flight."

"How are we going to get these old people to bed?" the nurse asked.

"That's your problem," Maria said. "I have to leave now. Another engagement is calling me."

"But you haven't answered my question." Nurse Maples followed Maria across the lobby. "How will I get these old people to bed?"

"Tell them a story," Maria suggested.

"But I don't know any," Nurse Maples said.

"Then make one up." Maria reapplied her lipstick while speaking. "Use your imagination. Surely you've got one by now."

Before the nurse could utter another word, Maria la Hija de Jesús made a fast exit. Relieved to be outside where the night air was crisp and the streets amazingly quiet, she turned her mind toward her late-night engagement. In one hour she would be presented with an *Outer Limits* award for best featured actress of the year. On the way home to dress for the occasion Mo decided to accept the award himself, but he had no idea what to say on behalf of Maria.

"It's been a long time since *I've* made a personal appearance," he said as Maria unlocked the apartment door. "I don't want people to forget who I am."

In the shower Maria's eye shadow and rouge ran together on her face. She shampooed her long hair, and while it was still wet, she twisted it into a matador's knot. At the dressing table the knot was secured with black pins, but her make-up was not retouched. Every drop of color was removed with creams and lotions. An electric razor erased a few spots of dark facial hair, and all finger rings were removed and put away. Then a white dress shirt was slipped on and buttoned. A black bow tie was securely positioned. Calvin Klein underwear replaced the towel, and black suit pants were carefully stepped into, zipped, and belted.

When Mo appeared again in the lobby of his building he inspected his image in a wall of mirrors. "I look handsome all dressed up," he said out loud. The sound of his vanity almost startled him. He looked around to make sure no one had heard him, and realized, with great relief, that the lobby was empty. He posed with his feet together, his back arched and his arms extended before him. "Now I know why I don't listen to my doctor," he whispered to his image. "I like being two people."

He adjusted the sleeves of his black suit, straightened his lapel, and assumed again the

121

familiar pose of a male Spanish dancer. Suddenly his acceptance speech came to him.

"Ladies and gentlemen," he said, as though already standing before the invited audience. "My whole life has been built on fantasy. I can't live without it, and I don't want to. Maria la Hija de Jesús has convinced me of that. She thanks you for this award and so do I. Only a few hours ago I came to realize that fantasy is based on an internal reality. Therefore fantasy trips are often more exciting than the real ones. And that, Nurse Maples, is the reason why I am an actress."

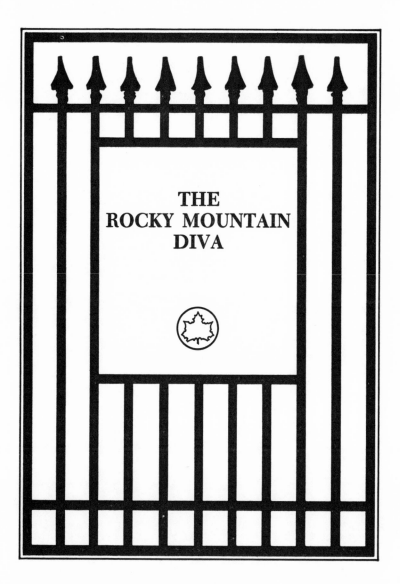

THE
ROCKY MOUNTAIN
DIVA

In a whirlwind of autumn leaves Katheryn Roberts stood in Christopher Park and belted out "Un bel di." Middle-aged, and overweight, she had somehow managed to squeeze into the powder-blue gown she had worn to her first recital at the University of Colorado. In spite of her hit-and-miss runs, her awkward grace notes and sudden crescendos, she was surrounded by devoted fans. Her voice, noticeably flat, soared above the noise of the traffic, several ghetto blasters, and an ambulance screaming toward St. Vincent's Hospital. Nearby on Carmine Street an Italian festival was in full swing. At 8:00 p.m., less than an hour away, Katheryn was expected to make an appearance there, but first she had to warm up in front of familiar faces.

On finishing Madam Butterfly's aria, she received flowers, applause, and *bravas* from her adoring public, mostly local music lovers who frequented the neighborhood piano bars and sidewalk cafés. Standing with the dignity of a saint,

Katheryn stared at a portable tape recorder at her feet. The recorder was spitting out a piano intro which was leading the soprano into *La Traviata*. "Sempre libera," Violetta's song of freedom, had become Katheryn's theme, and the aria which best represented her feelings. "As long as there are streets to sing in, I, like Violetta, will be free to sing whatever and whenever," she told her public.

Her street recitals always included an encore, the encore always a repeat of "Sempre libera." Although Katheryn's program varied from corner to corner, she never omitted her favorite aria, nor did she leave home without her baroque music stand, which she willingly admitted was unnecessary for practical purposes since her repertoire had long been committed to memory. "I need a beautiful music stand," she confessed, "like some musicians need a candelabra, or a velvet curtain, or a spotlight."

The music stand was used to hold an array of popular magazines—*Ladies Home Journal, House Beautiful,* and especially *Family Circle*—which she read to calm her nerves and rest her voice. She was addicted to popular magazines almost as much as she was devoted to music.

Unlike most street performers, Katheryn, who was born in Boulder, Colorado, did not accept contributions, only ovations. At her feet there was no basket or hat filled with coins, because she did not sing for money. Katheryn sang only for love.

Her unscheduled arrivals in Christopher Park were an event especially on Saturday nights when the cafes and bars were filled and the streets were packed. Charles Maplewood, who lived on Grove Street directly across from the park, was always on the lookout for Katheryn's sudden appearances. "Sie kommt," the baritone would sing out his window on seeing the diva stride through the main entrance like the Queen of the Night. "Sie kommt," he would announce over the telephone to all his opera friends, who were always ready to drop what they are doing and hurry to Christopher Park. There they would applaud Katheryn's flat notes, her uneven trills, and her wobbly vibrato that had, according to C.C. Wake, caused earthquakes around the world.

Katheryn realized that she had lost her voice. She also realized that she loved singing more than anything else in the world and saw no reason to stop. While warming up for her appearance at the Carmine Street festival, she took a moment to address her audience.

"If you thought Madam Butterfly was beyond my vocal ability, wait until you hear what I'm about to do to *La Traviata.* I don't know why any of you put up with me." This was her way of putting the newcomers in her audience at ease.

The devoted fans applauded Katheryn's little speech, causing her to miss her cue, and, leaping into the music, she rushed to catch up with the beat.

Shortly she would be warmed up and her ardent fans would follow her to the street festival. Traipsing behind her like Brunhilde's valkyries, they would soon pour out of Christopher Park like an unexpected cadenza.

"What did we do with ourselves before the Rocky Mountain Diva entered our lives?" Charles Maplewood asked a total stranger.

The stranger, believing that the question called for an answer, struggled to think of one. While he hesitated, Katheryn attacked Violetta's runs, trills, and crescendos with a sudden burst of exuberance that Charles Maplewood called "contagious."

"Oh!" he said to the stranger, "Doesn't she make you wish you were a singer?"

The stranger did not comment. During the next piano interlude he slowly backed out of the crowd while Katheryn, hands folded at her expansive waistline, addressed her audience again. "And now I will sing Lucia's mad scene from start to finish. I will sing every note that is written and a few that are not. As many of you know it was this aria that closed the curtain on my stage career."

"So sad," Charles whispered to the stranger who was no longer standing beside him. "You know she once had perfect pitch."

☙

Back in Colorado, Katheryn's vocal teachers had placed great confidence in her ability. "One day she will sing in the great opera houses of the world," they predicted. But prospects of a professional career came to an abrupt end during a student production of *Lucia di Lammermoor.* Singing the title role, Katheryn won the opening night audience, as she usually did, with the purity of her voice as well as her natural ability as a dramatic actress. All was going well until the mad scene. Katheryn, even then an unusually large woman, was amazingly light on her feet, but descending stairs had always given her difficulty. Dressed in Lucia's blood-stained gown, she made her way cautiously down the staircase, careful not to miss a step or a note. Once on the stage floor she relaxed, "perhaps too much" one of her professors said, and, giving herself totally to the mad scene, she thrashed about the stage in a fine coloratura display. The audience was enraptured, and Katheryn remained in control until the flute solo, which she echoed while racing across the apron as though searching for an unseen nightingale. On this mad tear across the stage, she misjudged her distance from the pit and tripped over the prompter's box, hitting her head against the stage floor and thereby ending the performance, as well as her career, in one misplaced step.

She suffered a severe concussion and lost consciousness for several days. After a month of bedrest she was still plagued with chronic headaches and dizzy spells. Her hearing was slightly impaired, and her pitch was no longer perfect. Usually a quarter tone flat, she was unable, even with intense vocal therapy, to regain her lost ability, but she kept singing anyway.

"If you stop singing for a year, your voice will return," said her vocal therapist. But singing was Katheryn's life, and no one wanted to force her to stop. She sang with tonsilitis. She sang with bronchitis. She sang with headaches, toothaches, backaches, and earaches. Nothing would stop her until she had strained her voice beyond repair and was forced to admit that she had irreparably damaged her vocal chords.

Depression set in. More weight was gained. At times she could not speak above a whisper, and finally Katheryn settled for a degree in music education. Upon graduation, she accepted a teaching position in Jersey City, where she lectured on music appreciation and directed three choirs which, like her voice, were always flat.

During the season she practically lived at New York City Opera as well as the Met. But lack of money was a problem, and she was forced to work as an office temporary on weekends and during summer vacations in order to pay for all the tickets she wanted. In this fashion five years passed rapidly and without drama until she met Howard Roberts.

Because of a rash of robberies in her neighborhood Katheryn decided to insure her home furnishings. She visited her nearest Allstate Insurance office, and thirty minutes later she left not only with a policy but with a dinner date for the following Friday. Katheryn had never had a date, not even in college. She had always been too busy singing or studying or making lesson plans or going to the opera.

"Do you like opera?" she asked Howard Roberts while they dined in Hoboken.

"I like everything you like," was his reply. Katheryn thought that was good enough and said she hoped to go out with him again.

Howard at twenty-seven was short, fat, and almost completely bald. His eyes had wrinkles all around them and the corners of his mouth turned up. After their first date Katheryn called him "good-natured and sweet." She towered above him, and he liked that. In Katheryn's presence he felt stronger, more aggressive, and more passionate than ever. He loved everything about her, including her singing. After their dates she would usually take him home, make him comfortable on her sofa, and serenade him until the neighbors started complaining and threatening to call the police.

"I'm just a dull everyday insurance salesman," he told her after dating for a month. "You'll get tired of me soon. No one ever goes out with me very long. They get bored because I'm too ordinary."

"You can't be all that ordinary," Katheryn replied. "Not if you like my singing."

Suddenly Katheryn discovered romance. Suddenly she started wearing make-up to school, frilly blouses, ruffled skirts, and perfume. She permed her hair, bought new earrings, and new shoes, slips, and stockings.

Suddenly Howard realized he was in love. The first thing he did was redecorate his office. A ten-year collection of food calendars with pictures of desserts, cheeses, and fruits was ripped from the walls and given away. Then he painted the office a pale but vibrant blue. Katheryn chose the shade to match his eyes. She also gave him pictures of herself in her favorite roles. He put them in silver frames and hung them everywhere.

Until then Howard had not been much of a salesman. His work bored him and he only sold enough insurance to meet his financial needs. But when Katheryn came along, he decided it was time to settle down and buy a house, and for that he needed money. Proudly ushering clients into his decorated office, he began selling more policies than ever, became the star salesman, and soon he was able to buy a small frame house in the suburbs.

Before he fully realized what was happening, he asked Katheryn to move in with him. She did, and several months later she discovered that she was pregnant.

Occasionally Howard's insecurities would surface. "People are going to want to know what you see in me," he said after they were married.

"Well, I have to admit," she answered without hesitation, "it's not just your money and your sweet disposition that I find so attractive."

Katheryn made Howard Roberts feel like a new man, and in turn he encouraged her to keep on singing. For a while they went to the opera together, but Howard soon became disenchanted with that. "Nobody sings like you," he told his wife. "I'd rather sit in bed and have my own private performance."

When Howard Roberts, Jr. was born, Katheryn said that he was the best accident that ever happened to her. On the day of his birth Howard bought himself a red sports coat and his wife a mink stole. A year later Michael Roberts, called "Bud," was born in a taxi on the way to the hospital, and three months later Howard celebrated the event by taking his wife on a two-day cruise to nowhere. "A taxi might not be the most sanitary place to give birth," Katheryn told her husband, as their ship sailed through Verrazano Narrows, "but due to the pot holes and lack of shock absorbers, our Bud came into this world in record time."

Having children weakened Katheryn's abdominal muscles even more and finished off what was left of her voice. Still, Howard begged her to vocalize every day, and she did. She would do anything to please him. Eventually she stopped teaching and devoted all her time to raising her family. She was what the popular magazines considered a model suburban mother. Her husband and sons were fat and happy. She starched their clothes, ironed them with care, and kept an immaculate house. Being a housewife absorbed all of Katheryn's time and energy, and for many years she had no desire to go to the opera and little need to sing except on Howard's request.

When her little fat sons were going on eight and nine, and her little husband was happier, fatter, and more successful than ever in the insurance business, Katheryn's desire to sing professionally suddenly returned.

Howard hired Madam Sokolova, a vocal teacher, to come to their home every Wednesday afternoon. "All my wife needs is some professional encouragement," he said. But after a month Madam Sokolova gave up.

"This is terrible thing," Madam said to her student. "Your love of music is immeasurable. So why you can't sing? So why God did this crazy thing for you?"

"Accidents happen," Katheryn explained the day Madam Sokolova threw up her hands and walked out. "Somewhere in this world there are lots of people who would love to hear me sing again. I'm determined to find them."

And she did, again quite by accident.

While attending the San Gennaro street festival in Little Italy, the desire to sing Italian opera became so strong she was compelled to stand on a high stoop above the street vendors, the crowd, and the amusement rides and belt out "Vissi d'arte" followed by "Caro nome." The crowd, in high spirits, cheered her on. Nobody cared that she was flat, that her trills were slow, or her attacks were ragged. The only thing that mattered were the arias. They had to be Italian.

"And now," she announced, "I would like to

135

sing Mimi's farewell from *La Boheme.* I hope you will all recognize it."

Her little fat husband, flanked by their little fat sons, sat on the stoop and told everyone that Katheryn would sing whatever they wanted to hear. Before long a large crowd had gathered around the stoop and the food stalls. "Just keep her singing," the vendors told Howard. "Business has never been so good."

Katheryn had no intention of stopping. While she belted out one aria after another, the food vendors brought her husband and sons anything they wanted to eat. Italian pastries disappeared into their cavernous mouths. Spumetti, biscotti, and amarettoni were served to the little fat family on palms, napkins, and paper plates. "Don't let her stop," the vendors begged as they plied Katheryn's husband and sons with cannoli siciliana, cannoli napoliano, spumoni, tartufo, and cremolata, followed by summer ices, granite di limone, granite di chocolate, and granite di arancio. Linguini and clam sauce was then served along with garlic bread, sweet Italian sausages, scungili, calamari, and pepperoni pizza.

As Howard and his sons gobbled and slurped and dripped onto their starched shirts and carefully creased trousers, Katheryn sang on and on into the night. Vendors shouted their requests and demanded encores. Old Italian women leaning out of tenement windows threw flowers at Katheryn's feet as her voice soared above the street noise, the carnival rides, and three gun shots that rang out from Lambruso's Clam House only two blocks away. There Crazy Joe the Horse was gunned down by a hit man hired by the mob czar Sal Milano. While the shots were fired, Sal, also known as Sally Clearhead Milano, was standing at Katheryn's feet while she tackled the difficult runs in Donizetti's *Daughter of the Regiment*. Next to Sally Clearhead stood his bodyguard, Carmine Three Fingers Ligotti, who refused to leave the festival until Katheryn had sung the death of Butterfly once again.

Hardly anyone realized there had been a gangland murder until the *Daily News* ran the story the next morning. Katheryn was pictured standing on the stoop with her devoted family at her feet and the mob czar and his bodyguard among the listeners.

"Our mother is famous," the little fat sons told all their little jealous friends.

"My wife is a celebrity," the little fat husband bragged to the Allstate salesmen in his office.

Before long, Katheryn's appearance at all the Italian street festivals from Greenwich Village to Bensonhurst was not only requested but required. With each appearance her husband and sons grew fatter, and happier, and more content than ever.

The crowd in Christopher Park had grown so large that people were unable to squeeze through the main gate. While Katheryn tackled the cadenza in Lucia's mad scene, Howard Jr. wanted to know why people sometimes laughed at his mother.

"They laugh because they can't hear her the way we do," his father answered with pride.

"I thought opera was supposed to be funny," said Bud.

"Only if you don't understand what's going on," Howard carefully explained to his sons. "Opera is very complicated, and it makes some people uncomfortable. And when they get uncomfortable they laugh because they don't know what else to do. If they had the opportunity to listen to your mother every day, they certainly wouldn't be laughing."

"This noise is liable to give me a headache," said Shelley the balletomane. She elbowed her way through one of the side entrances. "Charles," she said, adjusting her ballerina's bun. "Why did you make me come all the way down here? This woman can't sing."

"Her pitch may be off," Charles argued, "but she's a singer through and through, and that's all that counts. I know a lot of people who can match pitch but they aren't singers."

"Who?" asked Shelley.

138

"Let's just say a lot of people," Charles answered, "and leave it at that."

"You made me miss a ballet for this?" Shelley was furious, but she decided to hang around anyway.

At the conclusion of Lucia's mad scene, Katheryn dropped to her knees. Her hair was disheveled and her eyes were glassy from staring into the street lamps. When she collapsed face down on the cobblestones, a rain of yellow leaves fell upon her, and the audience went wild. Charles Maplewood had lived every note of the aria, and was now whistling through the applause and *bravas*.

Shelley was infuriated by the audience response. "People will fall for anything nowadays. Do you call that singing?"

"Yes I do," Charles replied. "It comes straight from her heart."

"I have married a good-natured soul who has agreed to love me and support me as long as I keep on singing," Katheryn announced while gradually regaining her composure. "Can you imagine such a thing?"

"No I can't," Shelley hissed. "Who in their right mind could?"

Howard stood up and took a bow. His bald head was gleaming under the street lamps, and the iridescent threads in his sport coat sparkled along with his eyes. He stood for a moment with one arm around his wife's waist and his head resting under her shoulder. "I look up to her in more ways than one," he confessed rolling his eyes upward. "So do our boys."

Howard Jr. and Bud were starving and anxious to go to the street festival, but Katheryn needed to warm up just a little more. "With your kind permission," she announced to the crowd now spilling into the street, I'd like to stray from my Italian repertoire for a moment and sing the Bell Song from *Lakmé*. I've never sung it in public before. Please forgive me in advance."

"This is only one of the most difficult arias in the whole world," Charles whispered to Shelley.

"Sometimes I get the idea you think I don't know anything," the balletomane replied.

Katheryn, folding her hands over her husband's little round head, attacked the aria with such ferocity and determination that the audience broke into wild laughter, applause, and shouts.

Shelley remained sullen, but Charles Maplewood, like Katheryn's little fat husband, glowed.

Finally Katheryn pronounced herself fully warmed up. To ward off the autumn chill she wrapped herself in her mink stole and marched out of the park with her head held high and her little fat family trailing behind her. Down the street they went, followed by Katheryn's devoted fans, who fought to carry her music stand. "I will sing the Queen of the Night on the way, she announced over her shoulder, "because once we arrive on Carmine Street I'll be forced to perform only my Italian repertoire. I do wish someone would find me a German street festival. My Wagner is improving ever so slightly."

"Don't tell me she sings Wagner." Shelley shook her head in disbelief.

"She sings Wagner," Charles replied, "like nobody else."

When Katheryn and her entourage arrived on the steps of Our Lady of Pompei, Howard wasted no time changing the batteries in her cassette. While he arranging his wife's tapes in the order they would be used, she addressed the gathering. "I will begin with *La Boheme*." Even her speaking voice carried to the top windows of the tenements. "You are about to hear Musetta's famous aria "Quando me'n vo'," which happens to be my husband's favorite."

"I like the music as well as the words," Howard said, "but especially the words."

"Please translate," Charles Maplewood shouted.

"But you know the translation already," Shelley barked.

"That doesn't mean everybody else does," Charles replied.

With her hands on her hips, Katheryn recited

141

the aria in English while promanading along the steps of Our Lady of Pompei.

"As through the street I wander
Onward, merrily, I wander daintily.
See how the folk look around.
Because they know I'm charming.
A very charming little girl . . ."

She sauntered back to her music stand and spoke in an audible whisper, "Pray, for Howard's sake, that I make it through this."

Her first flat note was met with enthusiastic applause. Then, confident that her audience was with her, she allowed her voice to soar above the noise of a ferris wheel set up in the middle of the street and a carousel going full blast on the next corner.

"This is *my* street!" Cherokee Rose yelled from her front window. "Go back to the park where you belong. We've got enough noise here already."

But Katheryn did not hear her. Attacking Musetta's aria with jubilance, she surveyed the crowd while her family and friends feasted at her feet. When people laughed at her sour notes and ragged attacks, she smiled, almost broke into laughter herself. "You have to keep in mind that this is the best I can do," she shouted during a musical interlude. "I realize it must be just awful, especially if you've heard the real thing, but I sound pretty good to me."

Shelley stood in the crowd with a scowl on her face while her friend Charles Maplewood remained enraptured by Katheryn's performance. "She makes me want to stand up there and sing "La donna è mobile," he confessed to Shelley.

"Then why don't you?" she asked.

"For one thing I'm a baritone, not a tenor, and for another thing, I just don't feel like a singer."

"But wait a minute, you *are* a singer," Shelley said, hammering a sharp finger into Charles's chest. "You've been singing in the chorus at Metropolitan Opera for fifteen goddamn years."

"But I've never *felt* like a singer," Charles confessed again. "And that's why I'm still in the chorus, and that's why I'm standing here on the sidewalk while Katheryn is standing up there on the steps. I don't think I've ever felt like a singer, not deep down inside. I can simply match pitch and sight read, that's all."

"Now, I have heard everything," Shelley growled. "I'm leaving."

As she forced her way through the crowd, Katheryn announced that she would sing "Sempre libera." "This is the aria that symbolizes my life," she shouted. "I have been known to sing it seven times in a single day." Missing her musical cue, she again had to rush to catch the beat. Her trills were slow, and her runs were uneven, but her voice carried to the top of the tallest tenement where old Italian ladies, leaning out their windows, were ripping up newspapers and throwing them into the air. The street audience cheered and whistled. Flowers fell at Katheryn's feet as she sang on and on, abandoning herself to Violetta's song of freedom. As she sang the aria that had become her theme, she was filled with great contentment. She was able to believe that her musical future was bright and promising. And once again her confidence was contagious. While in Katheryn's presence Charles Maplewood could accept himself as a gifted singer, capable of reaching great prominence. And while the audience broke into ecstatic applause, Katheryn's little fat husband was convinced that he was ten feet tall and the richest man in the world.

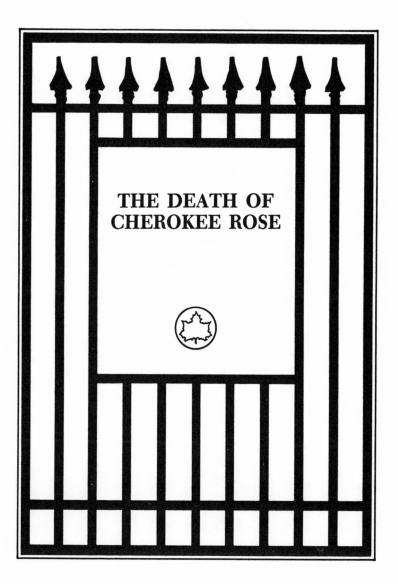

THE DEATH OF
CHEROKEE ROSE

Cherokee Rose died between the hours of 5:00 and 8:00 p.m., according to the authorities. The police discovered her body almost twenty-four hours later when five of her house cats, their hair standing on end, jumped from the bathroom window.

Shortly after Cherokee's death Wickie Wormser, who for the last twelve years had audited Cherokee's writing class, sat at the counter of the B&B Café on Second Avenue and wondered what she would do next. Helen, the waitress, had not yet noticed her sitting there. Usually Cherokee was with her. Usually they ordered two cups of coffee and two grilled cheese sandwiches before going to class, but that day Wickie would have to cut the order in half, and that worried her. She realized that Helen was going to ask her why Cherokee wasn't there. She also realized that she didn't know which answer she would give. She had not yet decided if she would say that Cherokee was sick or dead. She could not decide which

147

answer was the best. She didn't even know why she was sitting there.

By the calendar winter was a little more than a month away, but the weather was already cold and damp. Wickie, in a state of shock, felt chilled through and through. Suddenly it seemed as though an invisible curtain was separating her from everyone else. She didn't know if she was on the right side of the curtain or the wrong side. She wished it would go away, but she had a feeling that it would not.

Wickie was in a state of shock because at five-thirty, shortly before arriving at the B&B, she murdered Cherokee Rose. At the moment she couldn't remember why she had killed her writing teacher, but she certainly remembered doing it, and in a few minutes she hoped to be able to forget the whole thing. She was trying hard to forget, but she realized she was only pretending to forget.

"It's hard to forget something like this," she said. The waitress heard her mumbling to herself and looked around.

"Where's Rosie today?"

"Sick in bed," answered Wickie.

"Sick?" Helen poured from a fresh pot of coffee. "Must be the first time in ten years that woman's had anything wrong with her."

"She's getting old, you know." Wickie lifted her coffee cup. Her hand was amazingly steady.

"Old and forgetful." Helen leaned on the counter. "Rosie's time is almost up, if you're asking me."

"Don't remind me of that!" Wickie whimpered. "Can't you see I'm trying to forget."

⊕

For forty-five years Cherokee Rose had labored over what would become her only book, *Neither Here Nor There.* Upon publication, she was acclaimed as a genius by some critics and a fraud by others. From the very beginning mathematicians studied her prose for its numeric balance and algebraic formulas. Musicians found parallels between her cadenced style and the intricacies of a Bach fugue, while astrologers aligned her favorably with the stars and planets. She gave herself entirely to the creation of one book, a lifetime achievement, and after its publication, she dedicated the rest of her life to teaching what she had learned.

She taught at the University of the New World located on Second Avenue in the twenties. Her only class, The PsychoNovel, a Modern Approach, met five evenings a week at seven-thirty and was over when it was over, sometimes nine, sometimes ten, and sometimes Cherokee insisted on adjourning to the B&B Café where her students would drink coffee and read to each other from their works-in-progress. Sometimes they sat there half the night.

Cherokee Rose had many devoted students who audited her class year after year, but the most devoted, as well as Cherokee's undeniable favorite, was Victoria Wormser, called Wickie because as a child she had been unable to pronounce her V's. In class, Cherokee showered praise upon Wickie, as well as her famous father, Dr. Walter Wormser, whose latest book was a study of Grimm's fairy tales, *The Brutal Brothers: A Child's Garden of Vices.*

"You must read Dr. Wormser's book along with Krafft-Ebing's *Psychopathia Sexualis*," Cherokee had preached to her students. "You will never be able to write psychological realism until you digest this material and make it your own."

❦

When Wickie's grilled cheese on white bread arrived, it made her sick to look at it. While trying to force it down, she wondered what she would tell Cherokee's class. She wondered why she had ordered the sandwich, and why she was even going to class. She wondered if it would look suspicious if she did not show up. She wondered if she had left fingerprints on the plastic bag, the bathroom door, the manual typewriter, or Cherokee's new manuscript, that no one, except Wickie, knew anything about.

☿

At the age of twenty-five Wickie Wormser had discovered *Neither Here Nor There*. She was in the Jefferson Market Branch of the New York Public Library when the novel practically leaped off the shelf at her. She was possessed by the title. "This has to be the story of my life," she told the librarian.

"I sincerely hope not," the librarian whispered.

In two days Wickie reached the last page, number 1,915. After that first, but not last reading, she said to her famous father, "This book is going to change my life."

"What's it about?" he asked.

"Illusion versus reality," she answered. "But it leans heavily on illusion."

Until she discovered the work of Cherokee Rose, Wickie had considered herself a painter. Self-portraits, in the manner of Edvard Munch, had been her speciality. "What you do with paint you can do even better with words," Cherokee had assured her. That's all the encouragement Wickie needed. She began writing in a cluttered corner of her Westbeth apartment, where she lived surrounded by brooding self-portraits which depressed her. "A roommate is what you need," said her father. "Someone to keep you company

151

and take your mind off yourself." He arranged for a young woman to move in with his daughter, but after a week the roommate said that Wickie's nervous energy was too exhausting. "Haven't you ever relaxed?" she asked, while packing to move out, and Wickie, chewing on her hair, replied, "Define what you mean by relaxed."

Wickie had been a tense child, and she grew up to be a tense adult. She had never been able to sit still without wrapping one leg around the other. And she had never been able to speak without whining and wrinkling her face.

After her parents separated, her mother, Helma Wormser, then a professor of Germanic literature and now a political activist for lesbian rights, had thought that ballet might correct some of her daughter's social as well as orthopedic problems. At the time Wickie was only eight years old. Her feet turned in, her spine was slightly curved, and she gave the impression that her thoughts were so heavy her neck could not support her head.

But five years of ballet class only made Wickie's problems worse. Madam Pavlova of Atlantic Avenue (originally Buenos Aires) pronounced Wickie *hopeless.* "Bring me your tall, thin sister," she said. "For her I can do something."

Wickie's younger sister, Kathy, was a graceful child who became a highly paid fashion model and later a happy wife and mother of two sons.

She joined Wickie's dance class and was instantly Madam Pavlova's pet. "Watch your sister and learn from her," Madam would say to Wickie. "Watch how she floats across the floor."

"Don't compare me to her," Wickie would mutter. "I'm not stupid."

Wickie was overweight and turned in. She had no extension and no elevation and no sense of musical timing. Madam Pavlova was astonished at her student's lack of coordination. "For her, walking is difficult enough," Madam announced in Wickie's presence. "It is a miracle that she stands."

"I hated Madam Pavlova," Wickie once told Cherokee Rose. "I hated her as much as I hated my sister and all those other little girls who were so ethereal they could float away. I get angry just thinking about them."

Cherokee had encouraged Wickie to put her anger into her book and for twelve years she had done exactly that, rarely altering her daily schedule. She would awaken automatically at 7:00 a.m. and go immediately to her desk where she would write under the influence of coffee, chocolate bars, and frosted cupcakes. In the afternoon she would rewrite what she had written that morning and at five o'clock she would amble off to Cherokee's apartment on Carmine Street. Together they would stroll to the B&B Café for their daily

153

grilled cheese sandwich, and from there they would go directly to the School for the New World, arriving in class around seven-thirty.

Cherokee always started her classes by welcoming the special guests of the evening. "Come in, Mr. Joyce," she would say gesturing to the invisible visitor. "We have a place of honor waiting for you. Where is Mrs. Joyce this evening? Oh, Monsieur Proust, how kind of you to grace us with your presence. Please make yourself comfortable." Wickie would often give up her chair so one of the invisible guests could sit on the first row.

Many of the students assumed that Wickie and Cherokee were related because they seemed to think alike. They also resembled each other. Both were five-and-a-half feet tall with round figures and long auburn hair cut in bangs and falling to their shoulders. Cherokee's face was heavily wrinkled and Wickie, due to her constant squint, showed signs of early aging. Over the years Wickie had acquired Cherokee's love for long peasant skirts and East Indian blouses decorated with tiny mirrors. They shared a weakness for Afghan wedding dresses and Chinese slippers, hightop boots, and Guatemalan huipiles worn with Mexican serapes or old fur coats they shopped for in the thrift stores on the Upper East Side. But Cherokee's favorite outfit was a Ukrainian blouse worn with her Gogol overcoat and her Cherry Orchard skirt, presents from a costumer at the Circle Rep.

☺

"Thank God I killed her in her Cherry Orchard skirt," Wickie whispered to her half-eaten sandwich. Then she looked over the chapters she intended to read in class. She remembered that Cherokee always limited the number of pages to ten. "I'm going to read thirty-four pages tonight," she told Helen. "I don't think Cherokee will mind, do you?"

"If she's not there, how can she mind?" answered Helen. She was choosing her lottery numbers by rolling dice.

"That's just what I wanted you to say, Helen." Wickie smiled. Suddenly she was very hungry. "I think I'll eat Cherokee's sandwich now. I think she would want me to, don't you?"

☺

That afternoon Cherokee had asked Wickie to meet her earlier than usual. "I want to read you something I've just written," she said. "Come around four-thirty."

Cherokee's apartment was cluttered with theatrical props and scenery. For a little more than her monthly rent she allowed a local repertory theatre to use her spacious floor through for storage. Sets were safe with Cherokee, but costumes were not. She would wear anything.

155

"I didn't know you were writing again," Wickie said when she entered Cherokee's apartment. That day the front rooms were filled with backdrops from *The Beggar's Opera* and flats from *The Glass Menagerie*. For over a year Cherokee had been sitting on park benches from *The Zoo Story* and sleeping on a fainting couch from a musical based onthe life of Sigmund Freud. Tables and chairs, representing various periods from the Renaissance to the present, lined a narrow path through the apartment or hung from ceiling hooks. Curtains and tapestries divided the rooms, and all the doors were draped. Carpets on top of carpets covered the floor, and on them Cherokee's fourteen cats ate, drank, and sharpened their claws.

"I had no intention of writing another book," said Cherokee. "It started pouring out of me at five o'clock this morning. I couldn't stop it. Now I have three completed chapters, and if I'm not mistaken, I've found a new inner voice."

She led Wickie through the children's room, where backdrops from *Snow White* hung on the walls and stuffed animals with teacups in their paws sat in every chair.

"I'd love to go to sleep and wake up in your children's room," said Wickie.

"One day you just might," said Cherokee.

In the front room Cherokee sat on her *King Lear* chair, arranged some papers on her *Ah,*

Wilderness desk, and started to read. Wickie, standing on *The Music Man* podium which elevated the *King Lear* chair, followed Cherokee's long opening sentence down the page. Her lips formed the words Cherokee spoke. Soon they were reading together.

☖

Wickie paid for the two sandwiches and left a fifteen-cent tip. She never left more than that, even though she received an inheritance in monthly payments. "I'll tell Cherokee you asked about her," she said to Helen. Then she walked rapidly up Second Avenue toward the School for the New World. Her long red skirt dragged the sidewalk. Her purple shawl, draped over her head, afforded her little protection from the damp November wind. At seven thirty-five she walked into class on the third floor.

"Cherokee won't be here tonight," Wickie hesitantly announced. "She's not able to walk today. Don't ask me why."

Wickie stood before the class and wondered why she was there. "Come in, Mr. Henry James," she said. "Where is your brother William, tonight? We have reserved a place of honor for you as well as Señor Cervantes, who will be along shortly." She paused, as Cherokee always did, for laughs, but no one laughed. She wondered why they laughed at Cherokee and not at her. She

157

wondered if she should be doing what she was doing, and if standing somewhere else, she would be the same person. She wondered if Cherokee Rose had ever had misgivings, if she had ever wanted to be someone else.

☙

Every now and then Cherokee Rose had wondered what would have happened to her had she been born one-eighth Cherokee instead of one-sixteenth Cherokee. She had even caught herself wondering what would have happened if she been born Choctaw instead of Cherokee, Pawnee instead of Choctaw, or Blackfoot instead of Cheyenne. She had also wondered if her small amount of Indian blood had made any difference at all.

Toward the end of her life she had wondered what would have happened to her if she had made different choices. When *Neither Here Nor There* had been published, Frances Judd, the notorious critic, made a statement that had haunted Cherokee the rest of her life: "Miss Rose labored forty-five years on her novel. Wouldn't marriage have given her something better to do?"

Cherokee sometimes found herself wondering if Frances Judd had been right. Up until then she had never placed a high value on marriage or given it much consideration. Her mother, an actress at the turn of the century, had abandoned her at an early age, and her father, an East Coast

158

gambler, had never seen his daughter. Reared by her widowed grandmother, who read Charles Dickens aloud at the dinner table, Cherokee grew up loving long words, verbal rhythms, and complicated plots. Her grandmother instilled in her an appreciation for their small amount of Indian blood, as well as a reverence for the life of an artist, a life Cherokee learned to value over marriage, children, and money. "I cannot divide my energy," she had always said. "That's the reason why I am a solitary person. My work demands it." But in spite of what she said, she had occasionally caught herself thumbing through the pages of *Brides* magazine as well as *Good Housekeeping*.

"It's hard to get old all by yourself," she had confessed to Wickie. "That's why I sometimes visualize myself in a large white house with children and wicker furniture on the lawn."

Cherokee believed in the power of visualization, especially for the fiction writer. "Visualize, visualize, visualize." For her entire teaching career this had been Cherokee's constant advice to her students. "Give the inner voice an external form, and then let it talk to you."

Wickie Wormser had taken Cherokee's words to heart. She had never been able to write a sentence without visualizing herself wearing Cherokee's dresses and writing at Cherokee's desk.

"Visualizing myself writing next to Cherokee helps me put energy into my words," Wickie had said. But over the years her mental picture of the two of them working side by side began to blur. By then they had been dressing alike for a long time. They had been sharing the same clothing too. Before long, Wickie could only visualize one person sitting at Cherokee's desk.

"You're looking more like that writing teacher every time I see you," her father remarked on one of their chance meetings. Wickie, on her way to Cherokee's apartment, was wearing a magenta skirt with an uneven hem, shoes that did not match, and a dark blouse that was buttoned up wrong. A long-sleeved sweater was draped over her head and tied under her chin.

"Cherokee and I have become one," Wickie whined, chewing on her bottom lip as she spoke to her father.

"Lesbians, lesbians," exclaimed Dr. Wormser, scratching his head with both hands. "I'm surrounded by nothing but lesbians! First my wife and now my daughter."

"You're not listening to me, again," Wickie complained. Her voice was nasal and pitched higher than usual. "Cherokee and I exist on a plane higher than mere physical expression. Can't you understand that?"

"Go home and draw a circle on the floor and

160

sit in the middle of it until you find your center."
Dr. Wormser spoke above his daughter's protests.

"Nonsense," Wickie said, "I don't have time
for that kind of foolishness. I have my work to
think about."

She professed to be happy with her life and
the direction in which her career was moving her
and found no satisfaction in her father's mystical
psychology, nor in her mother's new-found hap-
piness, nor in her sister's undeniable beauty. Her
entire existence revolved around Cherokee Rose,
the writing class, and her novel-in-progress. "My-
self/Myself" was her working title.

Wickie called the book "psychological realism."
Her mother, the lesbian activist, called it "awful."

"My book is very serious!" Wickie railed at her
mother. "Your problem is that you have chosen
to interpret it on one level only. The main characters are a nun and a prostitute, and they happen
to be sisters. I guess you didn't understand that.
They represent positive and negative forces. I
guess you didn't understand that either. The nun
imagines that she's the prostitute, and the prostitute imagines that she's the nun, and they exchange clothes for a day. Then the reader, if he's
as sensitive as he should be, will realize that the
prostitute and the nun are the same person. They
represent a dual conflict within a single personality. Now I'm positive that you didn't grasp this

161

singular-duality because you still seem to think that I'm writing about two people when I'm actually writing about one and only one person. Now get it straight, Mother! "Myself/Myself" contains only one character. It just seems like there are two. Please, for once in your life, try to approach me with an open mind."

❧

Wickie removed the thirty-four pages from a shoulder bag and held them above her head. "Cherokee told me to read all this tonight," she informed the class. "She said our guest, Mr. Henry James, was anxious to hear this section."

Wickie sat down in Cherokee's chair and wrapped her shawl around her shoulders, arms, and hands. She crossed her legs, uncrossed them, and crossed them again until they were tightly wrapped. Only then was she comfortable enough to proceed. Her fingers, barely protruding from the shawl, arranged the pages on the table.

"As you know, I am writing about the conflict between the dark angel and the light angel." She wrinkled her forehead, squinted and grinned at her classmates. She could almost believe they were her students. Her front teeth fell over her lower lip as she spoke. "As you know, dark and light represent two sides of the same personality. Everything in my book is a metaphor. Everything has at least three meanings. Like Cherokee, I always use odd numbers."

With a lemon drop rolling around in her mouth, she started reading in a tight, sing-song voice. When she paused to swallow, her eyes bulged. She did not look at the class and was unaware of the students' restlessness.

⊕

Wickie Wormser and Cherokee Rose had first met at a publisher's party honoring the second volume of Anais Nin's diary. The night of the party Cherokee Rose was wearing what she called her Virginia Woolf dress and her George Eliot shawl. A white silk rose was in her hair. She always wore a white rose to literary events. It was her trademark. "This pale white rose was given to me by Na Na Shu, the famous Pawnee poetess," Cherokee told Wickie. "Everything has a name you know. I call this rose, Na Na's Pale White.

"If white, why pale?" asked Wickie.

"Oh, I like your mind." Cherokee quickly responded. "But you must realize that there are many shades of white. Pale white is pale white. Dark white is a darker white than pale white, or rose white, or gray white, and so on and so forth. The famous Mexican poetess Nanita Blanca has written eloquently on this subject. I strongly recommend her last book, *Muchas Blancas.*"

Wickie quickly wrote down the author's name and title.

"I was born in North Carolina," Cherokee said without waiting to be asked, "but I do not consider myself a Southern writer. I happen to be one-sixteenth Cherokee Indian. You might not think that's very much but let me remind you, Cherokee blood is very powerful. A little bit goes a long way. That's why you'll find so many images in my book."

Wickie knew all about the images in Cherokee's novel. "Are you aware that you use an average of fifty-eight similes per page?" she asked. "Did you plan it that way? Or did it just happen? Why are there so many earthquakes in your book? Why are there so many snowflakes? Why are there so many lakes and rivers and oceans and waterfalls and whirlwinds? Is it because earthquakes represent man's upheaval in the modern world, and water represents the womb? And if water represents the womb what do snowflakes represent?"

"The womb before it discovers itself," answered Cherokee.

The next day Wickie signed up for Cherokee's writing class. It took her almost a month to find the courage to read something she had written. But after receiving Cherokee's initial praise, Wickie's confidence expanded. For twelve years she read two, sometimes as many as three times a week. She would sit in class with her legs twisted around each other, her face knotted with anxiety, and read vehement tirades against her mother, who left Dr. Wormser for another woman. Through the voices of her one and only character, she would take her father to task for finding ominous meanings in her favorite nursery rhymes. And with long, oceanic sentences she would express her contempt for her beautiful sister, for prize-winning novelists, and all the publishers who found her work meaningless, dense, and laughable. She would also lash out at art collectors who had refused to buy her paintings, leaving her surrounded by her own neglected work. She cried poverty on every page.

In spite of her inheritance, day-by-day survival was a struggle for Wickie because she refused to spend a penny more than necessary. "This penurious existence is necessary to build character and strength," she told herself. "Besides, I need to save every penny I can because one day I just might need to commit myself."

Wickie believed it was necessary to experience insanity in order to add depth to her novel. She often worried that she might not be insane enough to be declared insane. Insanity had never frightened her, but insane asylums had. She imagined them to be dark and dreary places with militant nurses and masochistic doctors. After much research she read about Mountain Aire, a private asylum in the Catskills. "This is my kind of place," she said, poring over a full-color brochure. The asylum was pictured as a large estate with white wicker chairs scattered over the greenest lawn she had ever seen. She had a feeling that Cherokee would like it too.

Sometimes she would dream that she was already a resident of Mountain Aire. The recurring dream was peaceful, but it left behind spells of insomnia and bouts of nervousness. "During times like this, Virginia Woolf always saw a black fin slicing the surface of the water," Wickie said, "but all I can see is a big black bird swooping out of the sky and carrying me off."

The bird always separated her from Cherokee Rose. It never separated her from her family. She wondered why and often wished it would. And yet she lived with the recurring fear that she would one day learn to love her sister and live with her parents without conflict. That thought threatened the very foundation of her creative life, for like Cherokee Rose, Wickie believed that strife was the creator of all great things. "Without living under constant turmoil," Wickie said. "I'd never be able to release my innermost thoughts."

All of this she poured into her book.

✿

While reading to Cherokee's class, Wickie vis-

ualized Henry James, James Joyce, and Marcel
Proust standing behind her.

"What a melodious voice," she heard Cervantes
say from the front row, but she did not stop to
acknowledge his compliment. Without a pause
she inserted another lemon drop under her tongue
and continued reading the thirty-four pages.
Cherokee had written them that morning, but no
one realized this, not even Wickie.

✿

Cherokee Rose had been a firm believer in the
unconscious mind as the writer's most valuable
tool. "If you're going to write a modern, psychological novel you must be an archaeologist,"
she had often said. "You must dig down and find
out what's stored in the deep recesses of your
mind in order to write with your inner voice. The
inner voice is the expression of the unconscious
rising to the surface of everyday consciousness."

She encouraged her students to form an "in-
timate relationship" with their inner voices. "The
best way to get in touch with your deepest expression is to talk to yourself constantly," she had
preached. "Talk to yourself until you forget what
you're saying, and then you'll start saying things
that are important enough to write down. If part
of you believes one thing and the other part
believes something else, let the two parts fight it
out until the voice is one voice."

Wickie had made herself a receptacle for the teachings of Cherokee Rose. She had had no trouble finding her inner voice, but she had always had a hard time staying in relationship with it. That's why Cherokee had encouraged her to record her novel and then listen to herself reading it. "If you listen through headsets, you'll hear exactly what you sound like," Cherokee had said.

Several times a week Wickie had been following Cherokee's advice by sitting in a dark closet with her headsets on and her tape recorder turned up as loud as she could stand it. "This keeps me from losing my individuality," she assured herself. "It also keeps me alert, and Cherokee depends on me for that."

For the last five years Cherokee's memory had been slowly failing her. The names of her students, even the regular ones, had often escaped her. Sometimes in class Wickie had to remind Cherokee who was reading and what she had said about the student's work in a previous session. She also had to help Cherokee find her way back to Carmine Street.

"When you get old everything runs together inside your head," Cherokee had told Wickie. "I can't remember things as fast as I used to. I can't seem to locate my thoughts."

On the afternoon of Cherokee's death, Wickie, reading over Cherokee's shoulder, realized just how forgetful her teacher had become. The main characters in Cherokee's new book were a prostitute and a nun. They were sisters, and they exchanged places for a day.

"If you listen you can hear the ocean in my voice," said Cherokee, pausing between chapters. "Tomorrow I'm sending this to my publisher." Then she started reading again.

"You have stolen my characters," said Wickie. "But what's worse, you have stolen my inner voice." Cherokee was too involved in her reading to listen.

Suddenly it seemed to Wickie that there was no air in Cherokee's apartment. The odor from the catboxes was asphyxiating. Wickie became dizzy. She braced herself on the table while Cherokee continued reading. The prostitute and the nun were locked in a passionate embrace. Their clothing melted from their bodies. They writhed in bed, each struggling to annihilate the other, and at the same time desiring to become the other. Their cries of joy were cries of pain and their cries of pain were mixed with cries of pleasure. Their bodies became one body, their minds one mind.

"This book is just like yours in that it contains no humor," Cherokee said during a brief pause. "Humor would ruin us, don't you think?"

Wickie was too numb to think. She had never

169

listened to anyone read her work before, and she hated what she heard. The words seemed ridiculous and empty. "I hate you, Cherokee Rose," Wickie said. "Do you hear me? Do you even care?"

Cherokee did not listen to Wickie, she continued reading faster and faster, rushing toward the climax of the chapter. While the nun and the prostitute slowly merged into a new person, Wickie saw her creative energy being drained from her body and given like an unauthorized transfusion of blood to Cherokee Rose.

Almost too lightheaded to walk, Wickie swayed across the room to a floor lamp. A plastic garbage bag was protecting the silk shade. She removed the bag and staggered back across the room. Standing behind Cherokee Rose, she slowly opened the bag. She swayed to the left and then the right, and when she felt herself falling forward she hurled the bag over Cherokee's head.

"Let me finish," screamed Cherokee Rose as Wickie tied the bag tightly around her writing teacher's neck. Then she smoothed the bag over Cherokee's face and held her arms until they fell limp.

Suddenly the air in the apartment seemed fresh again. Wickie drew a deep breath. "Oh, I feel so free," she said, "Now I can go on breathing."

She left the apartment with the pages Cherokee

had just read, and as she ambled across the Village she read the first chapter aloud. "I like the way *I* read my work," she said. "But I can't stand hearing anyone else read it. It's just not the same."

☺

Only after she had finished reading to Cherokee's class did Wickie realize that most of the students had walked out. Three women and two men were still sitting among the empty chairs. Even the honored guests had vanished.

"I realize," Wickie said as she, too, prepared to leave, "that the forward thrust of this novel is hard on the reader's concentration because the theme is couched in so many understatements, undercurrents, cross-currents, and illusions. Please, no questions. I don't want to discuss this in depth tonight. I'm too close to it right now."

On Second Avenue a few early snow flakes had begun falling, but Wickie didn't notice them. She was too busy convincing herself that Cherokee was waiting up for her. She stopped at the B&B Café and ordered a grilled cheese sandwich to go. "I'm taking this to Cherokee," she told Helen.

"I'll send her a little something myself." Helen put a crusty doughnut into the bag.

On the street again, Wickie realized that the sandwich made her feel more secure. It proved to her that Helen thought that Cherokee was sick,

171

not dead. She looked into the bag to make sure the sandwich was still there. She touched it to make sure it was still warm. She pinched the doughnut to make sure it was real. "Whatever happened this afternoon is all right." She spoke into the brown bag. "It's all right because Cherokee is still hungry. This sandwich proves it. And this doughnut *really* proves it because I didn't think of the doughnut, Helen did."

Entering Cherokee's apartment, Wickie tossed her shoulder bag into a chair as if she'd come home. Cherokee's body was slumped over her desk, and the fourteen cats were sniffing the plastic bag or rubbing against her legs. Grabbing the cats by their tails and necks, Wickie hurled them, three or four at a time, into the bathroom. Then she arranged the sandwich and doughnut on a saucer and balanced it on top of Cherokee's typewriter.

All of a sudden she was very hungry again. She wanted to eat the sandwich, but she didn't want to deprive Cherokee of it. For a few seconds she didn't know what to do. Finally she decided to eat half the sandwich. She took small bites and chewed with her mouth open.

Having satisfied her hunger, she took off her clothes, folded them carefully, and laid them on a bench. Slowly she removed Cherokee's embroidered blouse and put it on. With extreme

172

care, she removed Cherokee's skirt and put it on also. Next she slipped her feet into Cherokee's slippers. She looked at herself in the mirror, but she did not see herself. She saw Cherokee Rose.

Now she was ready to move the body. She dragged it to a narrow couch and propped it up with pillows. Then she removed the plastic bag. Cherokee's face was relaxed and colorless. Her pale body disappeared into her long white slip at the bottom of which two tiny feet could be seen. "You're beautiful, like a pale white rose," Wickie said. "I want to be that beautiful too." She took Cherokee in her arms and lay down with her on the couch. Then she slipped the plastic bag back over Cherokee's head. She slipped her own head into the bag as well and tied it around their necks. With both hands she squeezed out the air and smoothed the plastic over her face. Soon her arms fell limp around Cherokee's body. Soon the fourteen cats, still locked in the bathroom, began to growl and hiss.

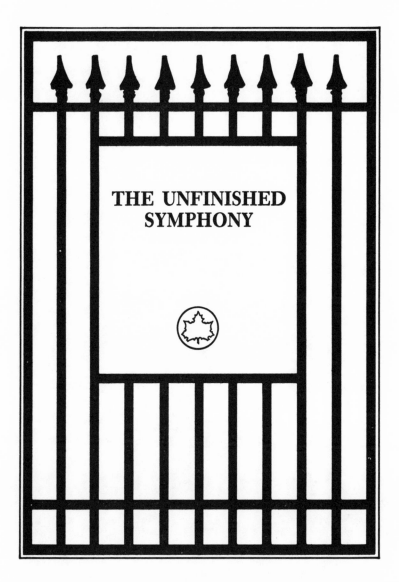

THE UNFINISHED SYMPHONY

Victor Lloyd Russell, the all-but-unknown composer (not to be confused with his brother Victor Lawrence Russell, the Nobel laureate) spent the winter of his ninety-ninth year in a sleepless state of anxiety because he could hear the last movement of his unfinished symphony, but he could not capture what he heard on paper. "If spring would only arrive," he kept saying, "I think I'd be able to compose again. And when I'm able to compose again I'll be able to sleep again. I just need to sit outdoors in the sun and fresh air."

On the twenty-fifth day of April, spring was still nowhere in sight. Mr. Russell, sitting at the only window in his private room at the Riverview Nursing Home, watched snow and ice accumulate on the sidewalks and streets. The late blizzard caused him much distress, leading him to believe that the spring of his ninety-ninth year would never arrive, but if it did it would certainly have to be an auspicious one.

"Something will happen to me this spring, that is, if we have a spring," he told the second-shift nurse, Joanie Maples. "But don't get your hopes up, my dear, I am not going to die. I'll probably finish my symphony this year and die next year. That means I'll be able to sleep the last year of my life. That might take a period of adjustment on my part."

"Why does it take so long to write a symphony?" the nurse asked.

"The verb you would like to use is *to compose*," answered Mr. Russell.

"Forget I asked," the nurse replied.

"Delighted to do so, my dear," said Mr. Russell. As he watched the snow fall, he heard music in the flakes swirling between the buildings and colliding with his window pane. "I can hear music in everything," he said, "I just can't match what I hear to the names of the notes I remember, that's all." The nurse was no longer in his room, but that did not concern Mr. Russell, for he had reached the age when he enjoyed talking to himself more than to others.

Having outlived his famous medical brother, his wife, and two sons who had become surgeons, he was now the sole surviving member of his family, and for the last thirty-five years he had lived in the Riverview Nursing Home. "When I first came here I could sit at this window and see the river," he said as he conducted the snowflakes with a pencil. "Now I can't even see the next street. Somebody should change the name of this place!" he shouted. "I said, somebody should change the name of this place."

Mr. Zemsky, the director of the home, stuck his head into Mr. Russell's room and reminded him that it was quiet time. "Very soon it'll be warm and you'll be able to go sit in the park again," he said. "We'll be very happy for that day to arrive, won't we?"

"*We* certainly will," said Mr. Russell.

Each winter he looked forward to the coming of spring when he was allowed to take walks by himself and sit in Christopher Park as long as he wanted. The other residents of the home were not allowed this freedom, only Mr. Russell. To get his way he had resorted to threats. "I'll call the police, if you don't let me out of here," he had said and had often done exactly that. Many times he had telephoned the local precinct: "Help! Help! They want to keep me indoors the rest of my life. Somebody come save me!" Finally the officers had persuaded Mr. Zemsky to allow Mr. Russell to have his afternoons of freedom.

During the warm months the nursing home would pack Mr. Russell a light lunch and away he would go down Hudson to Christopher and across Christopher to the park, where he would sit all afternoon.

But the spring of his ninety-ninth year was slow in arriving and this, along with his inability to compose, threw Mr. Russell into a fitful state. From the last of March until the middle of April there had been nothing but rain or snow, but every day Mr. Russell had persuaded the kitchen to pack him a lunch, just in case the weather cleared.

At last a fairly warm day arrived, and along with it came blasts of wind so strong Mr. Russell had to lean forward at a severe angle in order to walk the short distance to the park. He felt as though the wind was blowing away what was left of his memories, mixing them up and returning them to him in a new order.

"My goodness," he said as he sat down in the park for the first time since the last warm days of autumn. "I don't think I know where I am. Is this what I've been waiting for all winter?"

As usual when going out of doors, Mr. Russell was completely covered. His sleeves were very long and his socks very thick. White gloves protected his sensitive hands and wrists from insects that bit or stung. A fisherman's hat with new mosquito netting draped from the brim provided the same protection for his face and neck. Not an inch of flesh was exposed.

As he sat there peering through the netting, he could not rid himself of the idea that the park was different. Although there had been no physical changes, no cutting of trees or rearranging of benches, something just wasn't the same. He was beginning to wonder if Christopher Park *was* Christopher Park. The thought that it might not be disturbed him so he came to a fast conclusion: "Nothing has changed, everything is the same except for that section fenced off from the public. Over there, something's different."

"Who's that man standing on the other side of the fence?" Mr. Russell asked C.C. Wake.

"That's not a real man," said C.C. "That's a statue of General Sheridan."

"What's he doing here?" asked Mr. Russell.

"Just standing around," answered C.C. as he rushed to answer the telephone.

Sheridan was engraved in large letters on the base of the statue, but the letters were not large enough for Mr. Russell, whose eyesight had failed him twenty years earlier. "That can't be Sheridan, because this isn't Sheridan Square," he said. "What would Sheridan be doing in Christopher Park when he has his own private park around the corner. It doesn't make sense, does it?"

For a few moments Mr. Russell wondered if the statue represented his late brother. But he could not recall exactly what his brother had

181

looked like, and because of his poor eyesight, a photograph of his famous twin which he carried in his wallet served as no reminder at all. Mr. Russell simply could not bring Dr. Russell's features into focus.

That day, his first day in the park after such a long and cold winter, the identity of the statue perplexed Mr. Russell to the point of further investigation. Out of the blue the thought struck him: "If that indeed is the statue of Sheridan then this must be Sheridan Square instead of Christopher Park. And if I'm right, if this is after all Sheridan Square, then I've been sitting in the wrong park all afternoon, and possibly for the last *I don't know how many years* of my life. Maybe I'm lost and don't know it."

He then wandered around the corner to Sheridan Square, a small triangle of grass and newly planted flowers contained by an iron fence but without public entrance. At the end of this trek of no more than fifty steps Mr. Russell stood before a Parks Department sign which he could read only by lifting the mosquito netting away from his face.

"Sheridan Square?" he said in a loud voice. "This sign has *Sheridan Square* written on it. Have I been walking in circles or what?" He noticed, not for the first time, but for the first time in memory, that Sheridan Square contained no trees

182

and no statue. "Someone has switched signs on me," he said. "Sheridan Square is actually Christopher Park and Christopher Park is actually Sheridan Square. And if that's true then where am I supposed to be?"

Attempting to find his way back to *that other park around the corner*, the one he had been calling Christopher Park, which was, he was almost certain, no longer Christopher Park, a sharp wind blew Mr. Russell into a cloud of confusion. On retracing those no more than fifty steps, he lost his way and presently found himself on Sixth Avenue, also known as Avenue of the Americas.

"Where am I?" Mr. Russell asked.

"Avenue of the Americans," said a passerby.

"Sixth Avenue," said another.

"Nobody knows where anybody is anymore," Mr. Russell shouted into the traffic. "How did I get here?"

Maria la Hija de Jesús, standing on the opposite corner heard him. "Just stay where you are, Mr. Russell," she called. "I'll walk you home."

She was on her way to an audition for suntan lotion and was wearing a yellow sundress with a straw hat.

"Do I know you?" Mr. Russell asked.

"Yes, Mr. Russell," Maria replied. "You see me at the nursing home twice a week. I'm the one who reads to you."

183

"Oh!" Mr. Russell said. "Maria. It's you. I don't recognize you in yellow. Maybe that's it."

He insisted on going back to the park where he had been sitting and whose name had now escaped him. Maria, drastically slowing her pace, led him back to his favorite bench.

"I think that statue represents my brother," he said as they sat down.

"No, that is not your brother," Maria patiently explained. "That is a statue of General Sheridan. And this park is called Christopher Park. Don't ask me why."

"Oh, I must be losing my mind again," Mr. Russell said. "How do you get the clouds to clear?"

"The sky is blue today," Maria said.

"No it's not," said Mr. Russell. "It has to be cloudy because I can't remember a thing. Who am I? What's my name? I mean what's my *real* name?"

"Victor L. Russell," Maria spoke distinctly into Mr. Russell's left ear. Then she changed sides and spoke into his other ear. "You are none other than Victor L. Russell."

"Victor L. Russell," said a total stranger. "I thought he was dead." The stranger approached Maria and Mr. Russell. "Are you Victor L. Russell, the Nobel Prize winner?"

"No sir," Mr. Russell said politely. "I am Victor

184

L. Russell, the composer of forgotten symphonies. You are confusing me with my dear brother."

"You see, you do know who you are after all," said Maria la Hija.

"Oh, I'm so sorry," said the stranger. "I didn't mean to . . ."

"Not to worry," Mr. Russell replied. "People have always made this harmless, little mistake."

"But why do you have the same name?" the stranger asked.

"Why is Sheridan Square a triangle?" asked Mr. Russell, but the stranger made no answer.

"You see, Mr. Russell," said Maria. "There's nothing wrong with your memory *at times*. You just now remembered exactly who you are and who you are not."

"Well, isn't that something," said Mr. Russell. "I wonder if I'll be able to do it tomorrow?"

While Maria held one hand, Mr. Russell began humming one of his compositions. With his free hand he directed as he hummed. Pigeons, thinking they were about to be fed, flew to his feet. "Do you know what I'm humming?" asked Mr. Russell.

"Yes," Maria answered.

"What?" Mr. Russell asked.

"Your unfinished symphony," Maria replied.

"Why can't I finish it?" asked Mr. Russell. "It keeps me up all night long. All I hear is music going off in my head, but I can't get the notes to stay on the paper. They're floating around everywhere. I can see them and I can hear them, and if I could capture them I could finish my symphony, and if I could finish my symphony I could sleep again. It's as simple as that."

"I think you're not supposed to finish it," said Maria, "and you shouldn't worry about it any longer. It's just fine the way it is. Only you know it's unfinished."

"Sometimes I don't know who I am anymore," Mr. Russell managed to say while directing and humming. "Sometimes I think I'm Shubert."

"Shubert is a good example of why some things should be left unfinished," Maria said, glancing at her watch. "He would have gone completely unknown had he finished that symphony. That should be a lesson to you."

"You make me feel so much better," said Mr. Russell.

"That's what they all say," Maria replied.

She was late for her audition and nervous about leaving Mr. Russell alone in the park, especially that day. He seemed more fragile than ever, and she was convinced that he should not be wandering the streets alone. Many times Maria had suggested that Mr. Russell be accompanied to and from the park, but the director of Riverview had disagreed. "My staff is overworked as it is," Mr. Zemsky had said. "As long as Mr. Russell keeps finding his way back, we'll allow him to have his little afternoons."

"What happens the day he doesn't return?" Maria had asked.

"Then we'll terminate his little afternoons," the director had replied.

"By then," Maria had said, "he probably won't need them anyway."

For years Mr. Russell had been Maria's favorite resident, and she worried about him as if he were a child just beginning to walk. "Do you think you'll be able to find your way back home today, Mr. Russell?" Maria stood up ready to go to her audition but still not wanting to leave Mr. Russell unaccompanied.

"Yes," the old composer answered. "I've never been lost in my entire life."

"Well, just in case you ever are," said Maria, "let me tell you what to do. After you leave this park, walk west on any cross street, and the first wide street you come to will be Hudson. From Hudson you should be able to see the nursing home. If you can't see it, just ask someone to point the way."

"How do I know if I'm walking west?" Mr. Russell asked.

"Easy," Maria replied. "If you exit through the Main entrance to the park, you walk straight ahead. If you take the Christopher Street exit you turn left. If you take the Grove Street exit you turn right."

Mr. Russell said that he could not remember so many turns, so Maria gave him another plan. "You've found your way back hundreds of times," she said, "just allow your instincts tell you which way to turn after you leave the park. Then notice the house numbers. The numbers will get larger as you walk west. If you can't read the numbers, ask someone to read them for you."

"I can remember that," Mr. Russell said. "I know I can."

Maria left him to contemplate his unfinished symphony and hurried off to her audition. Shortly after she was gone, a cloud obscured the sun, triggering Mr. Russell's sensitive time table. "It's getting dark," he said. "Must be time to leave."

As usual he made his exit on the Grove Street side of Christopher Park. His instincts told him to turn right, so he turned right, crossed Seventh Avenue South, and kept walking along Grove. By stopping several strangers and asking them to read the house numbers, he came to the conclusion that he was walking the wrong way.

"Oh, no," he said to a mailman, "The numbers are getting smaller, and that means I'm walking east instead of west. How did this happen to me?" He turned around and started walking in the opposite direction.

188

"Wait a minute," the mailman shouted, after a moment of confusion. "The numbers on Grove Street run in the opposite direction from the other cross streets in this part of town. Hardly anybody stops to realize that."

Mr. Russell, contemplating his unfinished score, did not hear anything the mailman had said. Thinking he was returning to his nursing home, he walked back toward Christopher Park. Along the way he felt a sense of security in knowing that he was walking in the correct direction. Soon he began humming his unfinished symphony. "I believe I'll be able to finish it this year," he said. "I believe I know what it needs."

Presently he crossed Seventh Avenue South thinking it was Hudson, and a few steps later, he realized he was standing at the entrance to Christopher Park. Then total confusion set in. He started wondering if it was morning or afternoon and after convincing himself it was the next day, he sat down in the park and began humming what he could remember of his symphony.

On her way home from the suntan audition, Maria found Mr. Russell leaning over the fence that separated the public area of Christopher Park from the statue of General Sheridan. He was trying to read the inscription on the statue, but not even by lifting his mosquito netting and holding his glasses at a distance could he bring the words into focus.

"Am I in a cemetery?" he asked Maria when she tapped him on the shoulder.

"Would you like to be in a cemetery?" asked Maria.

"With my dear brother," Mr. Russell said. "I want to be next to him."

"Are you sure you had a dear brother?" Maria asked, somewhat surprised by her own question.

"I had a very successful brother," Mr. Russell said. "He was able to accomplish so much, but with me it has been a different story. My best work is not only unknown, it is unfinished. If I could only finish my last symphony I think I'd not only be able to sleep in peace, I'd be able to die in peace. All night long all I hear is notes, notes, and more notes. And do you know what?"

"No what?" asked Maria.

"It has just now occurred to me that they are all the wrong notes, and that's why I can't put them on paper. I can't hear the right ones anymore."

Maria, deciding to take matters into her own hands, led Mr. Russell to a bench where they sat down. "At your age, Mr. Russell, it is so easy to become totally confused," Maria said. "I'm sure you don't remember who you are, so I'm going to tell you. I think what I have to say will put your mind at rest. You do not have to finish your symphony because it is not your symphony to finish. So just stop worrying about it. You're confusing your career with your brother's. You're not the forgotten one. You're the winner of the Nobel Prize."

"I am?" Mr. Russell asked. "Are you sure about that?"

"Yes," said Maria. "You are not who you think you are. You are your brother."

"Oh, this is so confusing. If I am my brother, then what's my name?"

Doctor Victor, L. for Lawrence, Russell," Maria said. "You must always refer to yourself as *Doctor,* and then you won't forget who you are and what you have done."

"But I can't remember what I've done," exclaimed Mr. Russell.

"Remembering isn't always the important thing," said Maria.

"But what about my dear brother."

"Alas," Maria sighed. "He died before he completed his last symphony."

"I am not he?" Mr. Russell asked.

"No," Maria answered.

"Then what's my name again?"

"*Doctor* Victor, L. for Lawrence, Russell." Maria spoke first into one of the old composer's ears and then into the other. "*Doctor* Victor, L. for Lawrence, Russell."

A total stranger, on hearing the name, rushed up to Mr. Russell. "Are you really Doctor Victor L. Russell?" the stranger asked.

Mr. Russell was suddenly silent. Maria quickly spoke for him. "Yes, he certainly is," she said.

"Yes, I am," replied Mr. Russell hesitantly.

"You should ask for his autograph," Maria suggested.

The stranger thrust a pen and a piece of paper into Mr. Russell's hands and for a few moments Mr. Russell froze. "I'm not sure . . ." he said.

"Yes you are," Maria told him. "Now go on. Write your name. And don't forget your title, either. That's the most important part."

Slowly, Mr. Russell wrote: *Doctor Victor L. Russell.*

"My penmanship isn't what it used to be," he said, handing the autograph back to the stranger.

"Well, all this time I thought you were dead," the stranger said hastily, and then begged to be pardoned.

"You are not to worry," Mr. Russell said. "People are always making this mistake. You are probably thinking about my dear brother whose name is almost the same as mine. He was a composer." He glanced at Maria. She gestured for him to continue. "His last symphony," Mr. Russell said, "although forgotten and unfinished, is his greatest work and one day will be discovered. Now he's the one you should remember, not I. He's the one the world has forgotten."

When the stranger left, Mr. Russell entered a deep silence. "If I am not my brother but myself, then I don't have to wear all this mosquito netting, do I?" he asked Maria.

"No, you don't," Maria said. "It was your dear brother who was allergic to insect bites. Remember how his fingers used to swell when mosquitos bit him?"

"Yes, I do," said Mr. Russell. "He would not be able to play the piano, poor thing. He would sit down and hold his little swollen fingers and weep."

Twilight was closing in around Christopher Park. Mr. Russell removed his hat with the mosquito netting and then his white gloves. For the first time out of doors Maria saw his hands. His fingers were long and white, and his face, also pale from living under a hat for so long, was woven with wrinkles as fine as silk threads.

"Will you walk me home, my dear," he said. "It's getting late. I'm not sure I can find the way."

At the nursing home Maria turned Mr. Russell over to Joanie Maples. "I don't want to go with her!" Mr. Russell shouted. "Maria, find me somebody else. I want a real person to take care of me. Somebody who has some sense."

"Nurse Maples, I'd like you to meet *Doctor* Victor L. Russell," Maria said. *Doctor* Russell is the brother of Mr. Russell, the late composer."

"Who do you think you're fooling now?" asked Nurse Maples.

"Listen," whispered Maria. "As long as you call him *Doctor* you won't have any trouble with him."

"I don't care what his name is as long as he's ready to go to bed, and I don't have to fight to get him there," Nurse Maples said. "Come along *Doc*. Your room is ready."

As the nurse led Mr. Russell down the hall, Maria la Hija heard him say. "I'm ready to go to sleep now. It's been a very long, confusing day."

On her way out Maria encountered Mr. Zemsky, who had been working late. "I hope you're ready for this," she said, leading him back into his office. Mr. Zemsky, expecting the worst, sat down. "You've got yourself a new resident," Maria informed him. "His name is *Doctor* Russell, and he'll probably be around for another year—two at the most."

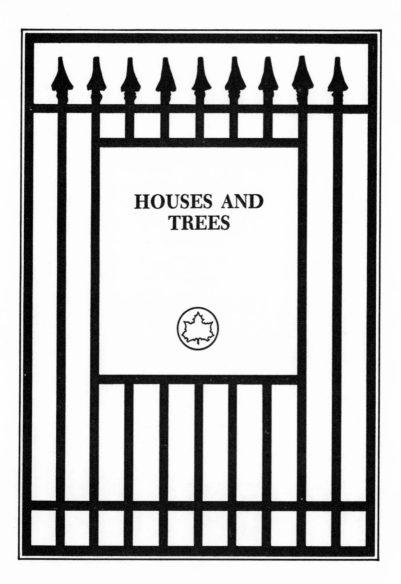

HOUSES AND
TREES

During a recent field trip to northern New Mexico, Dr. Wormser had invited himself to dance with the Pueblo Indians. First he offered his assistance to the women who were sprinkling corn meal on the ground, but they refused to accept his presence among them. Then he joined the Buffalo Dance with such abandon that the Indians were powerless to stop him. They backed away while Dr. Wormser, pounding the earth with his bare feet, almost lost consciousness and was forced to sit on the sidelines with the tourists.

When he returned to New York he said that every cell of his body had been magically transformed. "I was in direct communication with my animal spirit," he told his Jungian colleagues during a brown bag luncheon at the Clinic for Analytical Psychology. "The primitive overpowered me. As you may well know, I am one of the few white men to have taken part in a ceremonial dance. Therefore my sudden appearance was met

197

with a strong degree of hostility from the indigenous people."

"How did you calm their aggression?" Dr. Wally Subtable, asked drily. He was feasting on a tofu sandwich.

"My exuberance was clearly masked by an undercurrent of high seriousness," Dr. Wormser declared. "It became clear to my Native American hosts that I was not merely indulging myself but was entering upon my destiny."

"How, exactly, were you able to communicate your desire for acceptance?" asked Dr. Dorothy Bucher as she carefully inspected a rice cracker.

"I suspended my intellect and committed myself totally to the ritual of dance," responded Dr. Wormser. "At first I emulated the Indians' rapid footwork, and then I improvised steps of my own. At one point it became evident that if I stopped dancing the entire ceremony would have collapsed."

"How were you attired?" asked Dr. Henrietta Kraft, a visiting analyst from Zurich, who suspected her American colleague of undisciplined romanticism.

"Draped in a borrowed buffalo skin," replied Dr. Wormser. "The animal's head was strapped to mine."

Dr. Subtable yawned. "We will, no doubt, encounter this experience in your next book?"

"Certainly not," said Dr. Wormser, picking wheat germ from his white beard. "My next book will study personality assessment through drawings of houses and trees. In fact, I have already begun." He opened a portfolio filled with sketches. "A simple drawing of a house and a tree reveals more than a thousand confessions. The house represents the self, the tree represents universal knowledge of both good and evil, and the relationship between the house and the tree represents a visual assessment of the subject's personality."

"Study has already been done but without such obvious simplification," Dr. Kraft abruptly announced. "In Europe we have already made this advancement."

"But I'm talking about America now," Dr. Wormser argued. "And with that in mind, study for a moment this drawing by a thirty-three-year-old woman living in an urban environment." Dr. Wormser held up a drawing done in black grease pencil. "As you see, the house has darkened windows. There is no path leading to the front door, and no leaves on the tree's few branches. Dark smoke billows from the chimney and hovers over the house like a cloud of doom. No flowers are blooming on the landscape."

Dr. Wally Subtable stared at his tofu. "Perhaps the subject was deeply troubled."

"Obviously!" replied Dr. Henrietta Kraft, covering her salad with fresh sprouts from a plastic bag. "The denial of the child within. A classical case for which I would recommend sandbox therapy."

Slowly peeling an orange, Dr. Eugene Hydesmith came to his conclusion. "Subject out of touch with her own synchronicity."

"Unable to relate to the goddess within," replied Dr. Dorothy Bucher. "How long have you known this patient?"

"She was my daughter." Dr. Wormser spoke without hesitation. "I found the drawing after her suicide."

A collective gasp echoed throughout the room.

"You should have considered a less dramatic way of revealing her identity," Dr. Kraft ejaculated. "In Zurich we never form an alliance with shock appeal."

"Forgive me," replied, Dr. Wormser. "This unsettling experience is still most recent and unnerving. It has led me to make this in-depth study as a way to gain understanding."

He nervously searched through the portfolio while Dr. Bucher methodically stirred her yogurt, and Dr. Kraft contemplated her salad. Dr. Hydesmith had just lifted a spoonful of pine nuts to his mouth as Dr. Wormser held the next drawing in front of him.

For weeks Dr. Wormser had been asking all his patients to take part in his study. At least three afternoons a week he had also been sitting in Christopher Park, coercing the regulars into drawing and redrawing their houses and trees. Over and over again Dr. Wormser's sketch book had abruptly penetrated daydreams, interrupted conversations, and broken the concentration of those given to reading or writing in the park. "Just one drawing is not enough," he had been careful to explain. "A person's house and tree will change from week to week, sometimes from day to day. Often the changes are almost imperceptible to the untrained eye, but they are there, and they are very important. That's why I need many drawings from the same person."

Maria la Hija de Jesús was his first subject and a very willing one indeed. Her enthusiasm thrilled Dr. Wormser. And she enjoyed putting him on.

Maria's house was a cottage with shutters and a winding path leading to the front door, which was left wide open. "I am leaving this door open on purpose, dear Doctor," Maria replied flirtatiously as Dr. Wormser, standing behind her, strained to control his excitement. "Perhaps I will have a gregarious visitor this evening. I wonder if he will be someone I already know?" Maria drew a living Christmas tree on one side of her house and a bottle tree on the other. "Hanging bottles on a tree is a very old custom," she explained. "The bottles capture the evil spirits before they enter the house."

When he saw the completed drawing, Dr. Wormser's enthusiasm threatened to consume him. "So many symbols! So many symbols!" he exclaimed. "How can I thank you for your total commitment to my study?"

"Maria loves expensive jewelry," came the reply.

"This is truly a revealing drawing," Dr. Wormser explained to his lunchtime colleagues. "The subject, Maria la Hija de Jesús, is a Mexican transvestite who has become quite an underground celebrity. A star, as a matter of fact."

"Subject torn between material gain and spiritual wealth," observed Dr. Kraft as she methodically opened a box of raisins. "I am responding to the Christmas tree with presents on one side of the house as opposed to the bottle tree on the other."

"I knew this drawing would excite you," exclaimed Dr. Wormser, twisting his tie with both hands. "Now let me show you another one.

"The subject is an unknown composer whose late brother won the Nobel Prize in medicine. For some reason they shared the exact same name."

"The double," Dr. Bucher observed in utter astonishment. "Feet are not firmly planted on the path of individuation."

"Precisely," declared Dr. Wormser. "And yet the second time I asked him to draw, he drew one house and two trees and was convinced that he had lived his brother's life, not his own. Imagine, for a moment, the consequences of identity sharing!"

The analysts closed their eyes to contemplate the subject's duality. When they opened their eyes again, Dr. Wormser was holding up another drawing.

"Mr. C.C. Wake derives from a prominent Philadelphian family," Dr. Wormser explained. "He is obsessed with the study of fissures both natural and man-made."

"I see Greek columns," replied Dr. Hydesmith. "Subject is clinging to an ancient tradition which is no longer relevant. The cracks in the foundation tell us this."

"Why does the vegetation invade the house?" asked Dr. Bucher.

"What you're calling vegetation happens to be FISSURES." Dr. Wormser, startled by his colleague's lack of visual perception, spoke with indignation.

"Yes, of course," Dr. Subtable laughed. "Fissures in the universe."

Testing the sensibility of her American colleagues, Dr. Kraft inquired "In this stage of personality disorder, subject is concerned with universe. Yes?" The doctors all answered yes.

"In America," Dr. Kraft concluded, "everyone agrees with everyone."

"Now take this next case." Dr. Wormser, too excited to eat, held up a drawing.

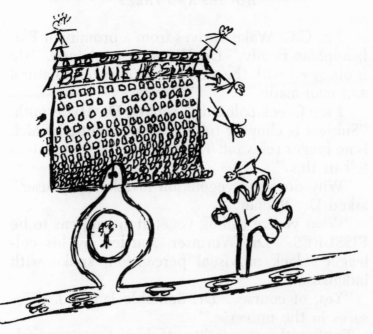

"The subject roams the city taking poses," he read from his notes. " 'Sometimes it's impossible to kill yourself no matter how hard you try' was her explanation for this drawing. 'Sometimes it's best to stop trying. No matter how high up you go there's always something to break your fall.' "

"Astounding," Dr. Hydesmith declared. "Subject is in working relationship with the process of termination."

"Not exactly," replied Dr. Subtable. "Only the aberrant personalities are being forced to terminate."

"Similar, in part, I would say, to Mr. McDay's problem." Dr. Wormser searched through his drawings. "Ah, here it is.

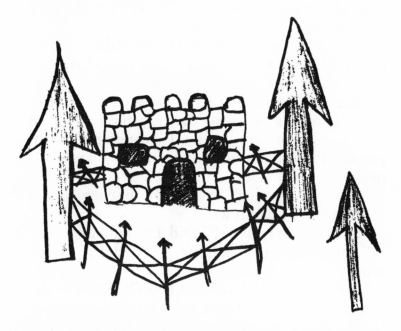

"I visited Mr. Clarence McDay at Mountain Aire, a mental institution in upstate New York where he now resides permanently."

"Trees growing outside fence of spears!" exclaimed Dr. Hydesmith. He meticulously removed the strings from a stalk of celery. "Apparently out of touch with nature."

"Trees suitable for warfare," said Dr. Bucher. "Perhaps criminally insane." Turning to Dr. Hydesmith, she added, "Celery strings contain most of the plant's nutrition, Dr. H. It is my duty to make you aware of this."

"Tell me," interrupted Dr. Subtable, as he folded his sandwich wrapper into a small square, "where are you going from here?"

"Back to Christopher Park," replied Dr. Wormser. "There is someone there who refuses to take part in my study. But I am determined to persuade him otherwise. At least I now know his name."

"And what is that?" asked Dr. Bucher.

"Andrew T. Andrews."

"Symbolic symmetry," said Dr. Subtable.

"Amplification of balance," added Dr. Hydesmith.

"The need to equate," capped Dr. Kraft as she extended her right hand. In her palm were four large raisins, an offering to her American colleagues.

✿

With the exception of Andrew T. Andrews the Christopher Park regulars avoided Dr. Wormser. If they saw him coming, they would run from the park without stopping to consider where they were going. But Andrew was not run off so easily. Throughout Dr. Wormser's field work Andrew had continued coming to the park at his usual time each day. For over a month he had been working on the last chapter of his third unpublished novel, and Christopher Park was the only place where he could think clearly. To protect himself from Dr. Wormser's constant interruptions Andrew had created a portable office from a cardboard appliance box. He had cut small air holes in the box, taped a flashlight to one of the inside walls and folded down the sides for easy transport. Dr. Wormser had often observed him unfolding his portable office and slipping it over his body. And on occasions when the doctor had ventured too close to Andrew's hideaway, sharp pencils had come flying like darts out of the air holes.

⊛

"Andrew T. Andrews has been nothing but uncooperative," Dr. Wormser said, at last attacking his Swiss cheese sandwich. "This will illustrate what I mean." While Dr. Wormser chewed, his colleagues studied a snapshot of Andrew at work. Only his legs could be seen protruding from his office.

"Mr. Andrews has found a method of calling attention to himself while withdrawing from the world around him," Dr. Wormser explained between and during bites. "Every day he sits on a folded newspaper under the roosting tree. No one else will sit there because pigeon droppings cover the entire bench. For some reason Mr. Andrews refuses to sit anywhere else."

"The subject is what I call an exhibitionist-isolationist," pronounced Dr. Subtable. "Were the subject deprived of his audience there would be no need to go to such lengths to establish his self-worth."

"Precisely," replied Dr. Wormser.

"Extraordinary," said Dr. Kraft as she examined the photograph more carefully. "The subject is living under and within his house and tree. There is no need for him to create a formal drawing." Unwrapping a piece of anti-plaque chewing gum, she assessed the whole project. "Study is unoriginal, but could be of minor interest to world of analytical psychology. We must see text to make final assessment." She glanced at her Swiss watch. "And now, colleagues, our luncheon terminates."

"But you haven't seen my Indian drawings yet!" cried Dr. Wormser.

"Tomorrow," said Dr. Kraft with finality.

As the analysts left the conference room for their afternoon appointments Dr. Hydesmith pulled a copy of the *I Ching*, with a foreword by Carl Jung, from the shelf. He opened the book at random. "How curious," he said. "I have received hexagram sixty-two."

"And which one is that?" asked Dr. Wormser.
"Preponderance of the Small," replied Dr.
Hydesmith.

Dr. Wormser no longer returned to Christopher
Park to solicit drawings of houses and trees. He
isolated himself in his office and even cancelled
appointments in order to organize the drawings
and write the accompanying text. After a week
of the doctor's absence from the park, the regulars
began returning like migratory birds.

By Friday afternoon, two weeks after Dr.
Wormser's last appearance, the park was back to
normal again except for Andrew T. Andrews, who
was still writing by flashlight inside his appliance
box. Without warning Andrew came bursting out
of his office. Cardboard flew across the park.
Pencils rolled out into the street, and pigeons
flew off in all directions. "I've finished!" shouted
Andrew. "The book is finished. I've created a
new language."

"That's just what we need," said Frances Judd
grimly. "A new language! I can't wait to learn it.
Give me at least twenty minutes."

For a while everyone in the park stared at
Andrew, and then, as if taking their cue from a
conductor, they resumed what they had been
doing. The Statue Woman, wearing a practice
tutu, was holding an arabesque penchée while

counting to 6,403, her new lucky number. The Rocky Mountain Diva was struggling through "Vissi d'arte" for the second time that afternoon, and Ellen Smith, who had taken up residence in the old McDay house, was memorizing lines written by a new playwright Mildred McDay had recently discovered. C.C. Wake was lecturing on a new fault line which he believed to exist along the West Side Highway, and Cameo Miller was counseling a housewife who had just called from Illinois. The caller's problem had to do with a compulsive need to organize and rearrange everything, including hundreds of decorative possessions.

Maria la Hija de Jesús was conducting a walking tour for six residents from Riverview Nursing Home as well as a few paying tourists. Needing a rest, they sat down near Dr. Victor L. Russell whose face and hands were uncovered. "Today I'm rereading my book on the Hong Kong flu epidemic." He held up his brother's book for Maria to see. "I can't remember writing it, and I can't remember what it means. That's what happens when you get to be ninety-nine years old."

"Ninety-nine years *young*," corrected Maria.

At that moment, a flock of pigeons followed by two scraggly parakeets landed at Dr. Russell's feet. While he sat reading his brother's book the parakeets chased the pigeons, and a stray cat chased the parakeets.

Andrew T. Andrews was oblivious to the goings-on in the park. Clutching his manuscript to his chest, he allowed himself to feel a sense of accomplishment. "I'm glad this book is finished," he confessed aloud. "I don't even care if it's any good or not. I'm just glad it's finished." He looked around at all the regulars, whose faces were familiar, but none of whose names he knew. "I wonder," he said as he crossed the park to introduce himself to the book reviewer, "I just wonder who all these people are?"

Not far away in his study,

suddenly at a loss for words, was asking himself the same question.

"Who are these people anyway?"

FRANCES JUDD

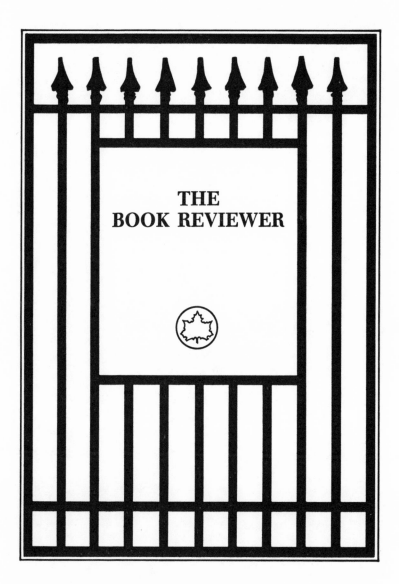

THE
BOOK REVIEWER

Later that spring, on one of those rare days when the sky over Manhattan was cloudless and the air was, or seemed to be, free of exhaust, Frances Judd looked out her window and frowned. "Oh no, another pretty day," she said to herself. "I'll have to do something about this." Good weather often depressed Frances. She preferred storms. Rain, snow, hail, or wind storms, she liked them all, just as long as they were violent. "I like to know that the weather is doing something besides just sitting there and being pretty," she mumbled on her way to Christopher Park. Her arms were loaded down with books to be reviewed.

She entered the park with a scowl on her face and sat down in the shade to work herself into a better mood. In less than an hour she had brightened her day considerably by writing a mean-spirited book review. On reading it over, she laughed out loud, frightening the pigeons at her feet and causing Andrew T. Andrews, who was proofreading his third unpublished novel, to stare at her viciously for disturbing the peace in Christopher Park.

"Wait till I get my hands on your book," Frances cackled. "You won't ever be the same again."

Andrew turned his back on her and went on reading under his breath: "Struggling against the equanimity of composure, I flounder restlessly in my unequipped expression of desire . . ."

While Andrew made very minor pencil corrections in his manuscript, Frances ceremoniously unwrapped a fresh razor blade and slashed the review copy of the novel she had just verbally slaughtered. She intended to send the mutilated book to the author along with a copy of her review which would soon appear nationally. Picking up another book from the stack of five at her feet she wondered, "Now just what I can do to this one?"

For many years Frances Judd had written nothing but evil reviews for three leading newspapers and two magazines. Specializing in fiction, she had never been known to write a kind word about a book or an author, and for that reason she was not only feared and hated, she was also read with amusement and sometimes pride. Although some authors suffered migraines after reading what Frances had to say about their labors of love, others believed that they gained a certain prestige from being taken apart by the infamous Frances Judd, also known as the "meanest woman in journalism." Many novelists framed her reviews or displayed their slashed-up novels on mantels, pedestals, and coffee tables.

"You just haven't made it until she's ripped you up," was the consensus of opinion among an established few.

"I've never read a good book," Frances Judd often said. "Furthermore, I don't intend to. A good book would probably kill me."

⊕

Frances had not always been a book reviewer. She started out as a psychic. Growing up in Jamestown, New York, in a family of spiritualists, she saw nothing unusual about table tapping, psychometry, crystal gazing, or spirits speaking through trumpets left lying around the house. Fran's mother read the tea leaves. Her father, a chemist, received what he called *inklings* that usually foretold an event, and her maternal grandmother was able to stare into the face of the family clock and predict the sex of unborn children. After the grandmother died, the clock stopped ticking, but on occasions, it would suddenly start chiming—always the day before a death in the family.

"It's a very sensible clock," Frances once told

219

her mother. "Because it only chimes before important deaths."

☾

"As a book reviewer who is hated, feared, and despised, I have some standards of excellence that nobody seems to know about," Frances shouted across the park to Andrew T. Andrews, but he was only half listening. "I review only important works of fiction by famous writers, prize-winning writers, or first novels that get raves from everybody else."

☾

"I believe Frances has a touch of the devil in her," Mr. Judd had said, shortly after his daughter started to school. "It's just an inkling I've been having."

Mrs. Judd had agreed. She had often gazed into Frances's tea cups and had seen many ominious formations of the leaves, formations she had never been able to interpret in words. "Fran's tea cups always give me the creepiest feelings," she had admitted, but only to her husband. "I sure wish I could read the message."

"I keep telling you, she's inherited some devilment from somebody." Mr. Judd's inkling would not leave him alone. "But there's nothing wrong with that. She'll survive because of it."

☾

"I have a reason to be vicious," Frances muttered to herself as the Rocky Mountain Diva stretched out on a bench. "It's my destiny. There's nothing I can do about it."

Katheryn Roberts opened a back copy of *People* magazine and watched Frances out of the corner of one eye while she read. The book reviewer was combing her salt-and-pepper hair. It was cut in a short bob and was perfectly straight. She was very thin and wrinkled. Purple veins protruded from her boney hands.

"That woman is absolutely frightful to look at," Katheryn said, burying her face in the magazine.

☙

In public school Frances had no friends because students and teachers alike had found her appearance unsettling. She was so thin her bones seemed to be covered with nothing but a layer of fine, white silk, exposing the veins in her neck, face, and arms. In contrast her long hair was jet black, and her eyes were pale grey.

She was said to be in alliance with the devil because she could make pencils roll across a table and glasses of water tip over by simply looking at them. Enjoying her notoriety, she practiced putting hexes on all her classmates and was accused of causing the Valentine Queen to break out in acne two days before the coronation. "I had nothing to do with it," Frances told her mother. "All I did was wink at the girl."

Her entire adolescence was marked by such events. She had a knack for predicting miscarriages, although some people believed she predicted them only through the power of suggestion. She made a point of talking about fatal car accidents weeks before they occurred, and she seemed to enjoy foretelling the deaths of beloved pets. Naturally no one felt very comfortable around her, not even the other spiritualists who congregated in the family home. Only Mrs. Judd and Mr. Judd felt safe with their daughter because her powers didn't seem to work on them.

"Somehow, where my daughter is concerned, I don't want to know the future," Mrs. Judd said.

"That's why you can't decipher the message in her tea cup," Mr. Judd explained.

Soon his wife was unable to read the tea leaves at all. As she gradually lost her psychic ability, Frances's powers took an unpredicted turn. It was discovered that she had a gift for psychometry. She could hold objects that had been in the family a long time—watches, brooches, or old hat pins— and after a few minutes of meditation, she could determine who had owned them and where the owners were living or buried. "This will be a very valuable gift one day," her father predicted.

Not long thereafter Frances was called on to track down a criminal by holding his cap. After a few minutes she said, "He's at the train station in Albany."

As it turned out, she was right. The robber was nabbed on the platform, and Frances was given the credit for locating him. Later on she was asked to hold a silver dollar that had been found on a murder victim. At first no images came to her, but after sleeping with the coin under her pillow, she was able to say: "I see tall grass."

Sitting in the back seat of a squad car, she pointed the way, leading the police not only to the scene of the crime but the murderer's hideout as well.

Gradually her reputation as a psychic became well known. She was called on to help solve murders and locate bank robbers in many states. Police departments were always sending her to some remote area to survey the scene of the crime and to pick up images from objects left behind. Her record of accuracy was phenomenal, and she was written up in national crime magazines while still in high school.

"I've had two lives," Frances shouted to Andrew T. Andrew while selecting her next victim, an author by the name of John Lewis Winn, III. "Not many people have had two lives in one, but I have. Put that in your book."

"Be quiet," said Andrew. "Who do you think you are, anyway?"

"The local genius," replied Frances Judd. "Now ask me a hard question."

◉

Frances boasted the highest IQ that had ever been recorded in the Jamestown public schools, so it came as no surprise when she graduated valedictorian of her class. "I make good grades because I know the questions you're going to ask," she told her teachers. "Even when you give different tests to different students I know which test I will get, so I only study for that one."

To the relief of her teachers and classmates, she chose to help track down a criminal rather than deliver the traditional speech at the commencement exercises. "I must get on with my life," she told the principal of the high school when she picked up her diploma in his office. "I have lots of important things to do."

She continued her psychic investigations into unsolved crimes and averaged a 75 percent success rate. Policemen became her first and only friends. She liked being with them, and enjoyed the attention they lavished upon her. Her father observed that his daughter was beginning to look happy for the first time in her life.

"I think I'll marry a policeman," she said, "I

have two already picked out, I just don't know which one I like the best."

"I believe Frances has outgrown her mean streak," Mrs. Judd told her husband. But Mr. Judd wasn't so sure. "I have an inkling," he said, "that Frances is going to have another career. It's going to be something entirely different, almost like a new life."

At the age of twenty-three Frances Judd's psychic powers left her. Plagued by pains in her abdomen along with headaches and fainting spells, she consulted a doctor who, as a last resort, recommended a CAT scan.

"There's nothing wrong with your daughter except fatigue," the doctor said, on studying the results. "Take her home and let her rest."

After a few weeks of bedrest Frances resumed her work with various police departments but discovered that she had lost her psychic powers. She would hold objects in her hands, and her mind would go blank. No pictures would come to her, no tall grass, no train stations or abandoned parking lots. She would squeeze the objects tightly and close her eyes, but she would not receive an image.

"It's the CAT scan," Frances's mother said. "I knew she shouldn't have had that dye pumped into her veins. That's what I was seeing in her tea leaves all these years and just didn't know how to interpret it."

Frances Judd sued the CAT scan doctor for a million dollars and lost. "What you don't understand," she ranted to the press, "is that this doctor has ruined my career and robbed me of all my friends in the police departments. He has also ruined my chances of marrying into my profession because I no longer have a profession. Psychics should never be given CAT scans. This is something that every doctor should know. I have half a mind to bomb that man's office."

☺

"I know how to make bombs," Frances told C.C. Wake who was preaching earthquake theories at the entrance to Christopher Park. "If you don't shut up I'll make one for you. I know how it's done. There are books on this subject, and I've read them."

"Bombs cause the earth to shake," C.C. calmly informed the book reviewer. "Bombs go off."

"You bet they do," Frances agreed. "I'm glad somebody realizes that. They aren't hard to make either. All you need is an active imagination, a pen, and a piece of paper."

☺

After losing the law suit, Frances decided to move to the city, where no one knew her. She took a room in the Village Hotel and got a job at a midtown bookstore where she sat behind the information desk and directed customers, answered questions, and made refunds. It was not always an easy job. The lunch-hour customers were particularly demanding. They expected immediate service and at times Frances lost her ability to cope. She would then slide like melting butter out of her chair and hide under the Information Desk with her dress pulled up over her head.

"When I pull my dress over my head, I become invisible," she told her manager. He suggested she find another job, but she refused to take him seriously and remained at the bookstore for ten years, becoming something of an authority on contemporary fiction. She could remember prices, titles, publishers, authors, and pubdates. She could remember plots, character names, and page numbers. In short, she became a walking *Books in Print,* and a fixture in the store.

When her job became stale and predictable, she slowly moved into book reviewing. "When I'm at the Information Desk I have no say in things," she told her manager. "The customer is always right, and my opinion doesn't count. But when I review books I get to say exactly what I think, and the author is *never* right."

"Books in the News," a fifteen-minute radio show airing once a week, launched her as a critic.

She recorded her scathing reviews in her hotel room and sent the tapes to the radio station. She never appeared in person, and at the store she stopped using her real name with customers. Soon she was asked to write a monthly column, and then a weekly column, and then a daily column on books and authors. She vented her anger on everyone and every conceivable subject, and still she had more anger to vent.

✿

"I don't have to open a book to know if it's good or bad," Frances announced as the pigeons flew back into the park. "I already know in advance that I'll hate it."

Andrew T. Andrews looked up from his proofreading. "I have a book you won't hate," he informed her.

"Oh yes I will," Frances said. "Just bring that thing over here if you don't believe me."

Andrew deposited his 800-page manuscript on Frances's lap. She looked down at it with disdain and spat on the title page. "I always begin by spitting," she explained. "So don't think you're getting special treatment."

Andrew, watching for the slightest sign of approval, sat next to her while she read. First she smirked. Then she growled and stomped her feet. "No one should be allowed to write like this," she shouted, shaking her fists in Andrew's face.

228

"One day you'll be murdered if you go on giving yourself to this sort of garbage."

Leaping to her feet, she read aloud:

"Focusing on existing foundations for improvement, the subliminal desire for success through which man becomes his best and most mutual friend, rises not falls . . ."

"Where are the characters?" Frances screamed, pacing in front of Andrew. "I've read ten pages and not a human being on any of them. You must have a character on the first page. Ideas are not enough. Any idiot knows that."

"But I've created a new language and a new form." Andrew, eager to defend himself, stood up ready to lecture on his theories, but Frances forced him to sit down again.

"You call this *language?* She read a paragraph directly into his face.

"Harboring the desire for self-sufficient knowledge leads toward the effective use of equations to express what cannot be expressed. In other words, the sum total of infant reasoning passed through the sphere of universal understanding is the equivalent of one's imagination squared."

"The name of this novel is *Totally Stupid!*" Frances shrieked. Her face was purple, and the dark veins in her neck protruded. "The name of this author is Bonehead! The name of this subject matter is Ignorance Squared! After you read my review you will never, I mean *never,* be able to show your face in public."

The veins in her face and neck were throbbing. Andrew T. Andrews could almost feel them pulsating. "You better sit down," he warned her. "You're too excited."

"Don't tell me what to do." Frances was beside herself. "I've never read anything like this in my life. Furthermore, I don't ever intend to again."

Shaking with anger, Frances collapsed on the bench. Suddenly she was very cold. "I knew when I looked out the window this morning that this wasn't going to be a good day for me," she said in a pinched voice, her lips bearly moving. "Somehow I just knew."

For a long time she was silent, her arms wrapped around Andrew's book. Realizing that something terrible had happened, Andrew picked up a pigeon feather and held it under her nose. The feather did not move. He blew on the feather to make sure it was capable of moving, and when he saw that it was, he held it under Frances's nose again. And again the feather did not move.

"Call an ambulance," Andrew shouted as Doctor Victor L. Russell wandered into the park and Cameo Miller, unaware of what was going on behind her, relieved C.C. Wake of his telephone duty. The Rocky Mountain Diva ran to find a policeman.

230

When the ambulance arrived Frances was still clutching the manuscript. "That's my new book, and I can't let it out of my sight," Andrew said, climbing into the ambulance behind the stretcher and paramedics.

At St. Vincent's Hospital it took two doctors to force the manuscript from Frances Judd's rigid arms.

"I've heard of this woman," one of the doctors said. "They used to call her the meanest woman in journalism."

"They still do," a nurse told him. "It'll be a long time before anyone will forget her."

The next day Frances Judd's photograph appeared on the front page of the *Daily News*, and under it was a brief caption:

"Frances Judd, notoriously critical book reviewer, died yesterday in a downtown park while reading the manuscript of an acquaintance. It is believed that the book, which had to be pried from her arms, contributed to her sudden heart failure. Throughout her career, Ms. Judd, who has never been known to write a favorable review, said that a good book might kill her. Apparently, that's exactly what happened."

A few days after Frances Judd's death, a literary agent tracked Andrew down and offered to represent the "killer manuscript" sight unseen. Quickly the book made the rounds to all the senior editors, but no one could agree on what Andrew had done. No one could determine who the main character was, if there was one, or what the theme might be. For that matter, no one could decipher the symbols and the sudden bursts of baby talk mixed in with references to higher mathematics. The title, *Marginal Footing*, did nothing but confuse everyone all the more, but, in spite of these drawbacks, Andrew's novel sold for a handsome sum, and was rushed into print. In less than six weeks it appeared in the stores under a new title: *The Book that Killed Frances Judd.*

Overnight, Andrew T. Andrews became a literary celebrity, and everyone wanted to interview him. "At the moment I'm too busy to talk about my novel," he told the reporters. "But if you want to come down to Christopher Park on any afternoon you can watch me write. I enjoy working in the public eye."

Andrew's next book, *The Biography of Frances Judd*, was already in progress. Maria la Hija de Jesús gave him the idea, and Mildred McDay agreed to organize his research. She located Frances's aged parents as well as many people who had known her well: policemen, schoolteachers and classmates, criminals and novelists who had been at her mercy. Even the CAT scan doctor agreed to an interview. Mildred spent every morning on the telephone tracking down anyone who might have exchanged even a few words with Frances. Booksellers and customers, cashiers in her neighborhood, radio personalities, newspaper men and garbage collectors, one by one Mildred McDay sent them to Christopher Park.

"If you can't make it to the park," Mildred would carefully explain, "just call this number any afternoon between one and three o'clock. It's the Earthquake Headquarters of Lower Manhattan. Someone will always answer, even if it's raining."

THE PARK

THE PARK

On the small end of the Christopher Park triangle there is a plaque embedded in the cobblestones. Because the statue of Sheridan takes predominance, the plaque usually goes unnoticed. It is inscribed with these words:

THIS PARK IS KEPT LIVING
IN FOND REMEMBERANCE
OF THOSE WHOM WE
HAVE LOVED LONG SINCE,
AND LOST AWHILE.

Mildred McDay was recently sitting in the park when a young man from the Midwest sat down near her. He had come to New York to establish himself as a novelist. "Why did you choose to sit in this park?" Mildred wanted to know.

"To be in the presence of the past," the young man said. "Many of my favorite writers have sat here."

"The past is not to be forgotten," Mildred said,

"as that plaque over there will tell you, but neither is the present."

The young man was silent, his eyes riveted to Mildred's.

"It's true, people have found themselves here," she said, as Cameo Miller answered the telephone. Her voice followed Dr. Russell into the park and interrupted Andrew T. Andrews, who was scribbling furiously. "And people go on finding themselves here, or losing themselves here, or in some cases dying here."

"People have died here?" asked the young man.

"Oh, I like you already," said Mildred, "because you have curiosity. I can see it in your eyes. Yes, people have died in this park and will go on dying here, and occasionally they return to pay respect to the living. Two nights ago, for example, Maria la Hija saw Frances Judd sitting in the roosting tree. Before that she glimpsed Cherokee Rose in her long white slip floating above General Sheridan. So you see, the past continues to live on, but for me it's the present that is so very important. People keep coming to this park because they can get up and say or do whatever they wish. Here they can argue and create and preach their opinions freely. And many of them, some talented and some not, establish careers in this little triangle, careers that have been denied them everywhere else."

"Hojotoho! Hojotoho!" sang the Rocky Mountain Diva as she entered the park to practice her Wagner. Her voice carried to Charles Maplewood's apartment. "How can she sing that aria without a spear?" he said, running his kitchen broom to the diva's side. She brandished the broom mightily while working her way through Brunnhilde's aria.

"See what I mean?" Mildred said as the Statue Woman posed in her tutu and C.C. Wake lectured on a tremor that had awakened him during the night. "There's a sense of freedom in this park, and it's not just the past that's creating it either.

"By the way," she asked the young man, "do you know where I can find a German Street festival? Somewhere in this city there's got to be one."

⊛